What A Delicious-Looking Guy!

Tall, wide-shouldered, broad-chested . . . Clover took a hasty assessment and rated this sleepy-eyed dream a resounding ten. Lots of black hair, some of it in his eyes, a ruggedly handsome face and a great body covered by a pair of unbuttoned, low-slung jeans and nothing else. Yes, indeed, definitely a ten.

"Hi," she said with a lot more enthusiasm than she'd arrived with. "I'm Clover Dove."

She watched the guy's eyes move down her body, then up again.

"Come on in." He held the door open.

"Wait a minute!" No way was she going into that house. No way! Not after that simmering, inch-by-inch inspection. Maybe he was trustworthy, but maybe he wasn't. . . .

Dear Reader,

Welcome to March! Spring is in the air. The birds are chirping, the bees are buzzing . . . and men and women all over the world are thinking about—love.

Here at Silhouette Desire we take love *very* seriously. We're committed to bringing you six terrific stories all about love each and every month of the year, and this March is no exception.

Let's start with March's *Man of the Month* by Jackie Merritt. It's called *Tennessee Waltz,* and I know you're going to love this story. Next, Naomi Horton returns with *Chastity's Pirate.* (How can you resist a book with a title like this? You just *can't!*) And look for books by Anne Marie Winston, Barbara McCauley, Justine Davis and new-to-Desire Kat Adams.

And in months to come, some of your very favorite authors are coming your way. Look for sensuous romances from the talented pens of Dixie Browning, Lass Small, Cait London, Barbara Boswell . . . just to name a few.

So go wild with Desire, and start thinking about love.

All the best,

Lucia Macro
Senior Editor

JACKIE MERRITT

TENNESSEE WALTZ

SILHOUETTE *Desire*®

Published by Silhouette Books New York

America's Publisher of Contemporary Romance

SILHOUETTE BOOKS
300 East 42nd St., New York, N.Y. 10017

TENNESSEE WALTZ

Copyright © 1993 by Carolyn Joyner

All rights reserved. Except for use in any review, the reproduction or utilization of this work in whole or in part in any form by any electronic, mechanical or other means, now known or hereafter invented, including xerography, photocopying and recording, or in any information storage or retrieval system, is forbidden without the permission of the publisher, Silhouette Books, 300 E. 42nd St., New York, N.Y. 10017

ISBN: 0-373-05774-1

First Silhouette Books printing March 1993

All the characters in this book have no existence outside the imagination of the author and have no relation whatsoever to anyone bearing the same name or names. They are not even distantly inspired by any individual known or unknown to the author, and all incidents are pure invention.

® and ™: Trademarks used with authorization. Trademarks indicated with ® are registered in the United States Patent and Trademark Office, the Canada Trade Mark Office and in other countries.

Printed in the U.S.A.

JACKIE MERRITT

and her husband live just outside of Las Vegas, Nevada. An accountant for many years, Jackie has happily traded numbers for words. Next to family, books are her greatest joy, both for reading and writing.

One

___

Clover Dove knew better than most that some people desperately needed to feel unique and did everything in their power to achieve it, since her own parents fell into that rather questionable category. Who could ever cause more wide-eyed adoration than her father, Billy Dove? And who could possibly raise more eyebrows than her mother, Francine?

Billy and Francine Dove were quite a pair. They fought all over the headlines and sometimes reconciled in crowded, well-known bistros, creating more headlines. And the country music fans ate it all up. It was a toss-up as to who was the most popular, Billy or Francine. It was rare when each of them didn't have a record near the top of the country music charts, and the competition was fierce between them. They never performed on the same stage at the same time because they couldn't stay friendly long enough to put a show together.

As the only child of two such volatile people, Clover had become a peacemaker at a very early age. She was still doing it, she thought with a sigh, this time at Francine's bidding.

"You have got to go out to Pudge's hideaway and see how your father is doing. I'm sure that's where he is. Something's wrong, Baby. He's canceled two concerts, and Billy Dove doesn't cancel concerts for no reason."

If that weren't so true, Clover wouldn't be on her way to a place she'd never been invited to visit. The Tennessee back road was devoid of traffic, but the unusually hard rain was keeping her alert. It was late, after midnight. At her mother's insistence—and no one could insist on something the way Francine could—Clover had left for Pudge Lang's "hideaway" the minute she got out of the rehearsal session. The director had announced a week's break, so she had felt free to leave the city.

Unlike Francine and Billy, Clover's ambition—or lack thereof—pretty much confined her musical career to singing backup for more enthusiastic performers. She had a good voice but absolutely no desire to make a recording of her own. Besides, she wouldn't need the money earned from such an endeavor if she lived to be two hundred years old. Francine and Billy had set up so many trusts and funds for their daughter that Clover had a hard time keeping track of them.

As for fame, forget it. She'd seen all of her life what fame could do to people. And not with just her own weird parents, either. Did she even know any normal people in the business?

Well, there were some, she had to admit. But few people denied that entertainers were a strange lot. They were driven to perform, craving applause and acclamation more than food or drink. And Clover wanted no part of it. Her fondest dream was to find a normal, anonymous man and get married, have normal, anonymous children, and live in a normal, anonymous town. Or in the country. A farm would be even better than a house in town. A normal, anonymous farm, of course.

Escaping the "Dove" name was impossible, though. Unless she disguised herself, changed her name and made a clean and total break with her parents, there was no way to become Ms. Normal and Anonymous. Clover had pondered doing just that, but she loved her fruitcake mother and father, and she was certainly the apple of their eye, whatever they felt for each other.

That was always the rub for Clover: what Billy and Francine thought of each other. There had to be love between them; why else would they bother to fight and make up so often? The peace never lasted for long, but it was the peaceful times Clover cherished and couldn't forgo, not even for her own dreams.

Clover was an undoubtable combination of Billy and Francine. As the product of two outstandingly good-looking people, Clover had inherited her mother's bottle-green eyes and her father's almost platinum blond hair. Francine's hair was a garish red, made a little more garish in the past few years by a hairdresser with a flair for the dramatic. Billy was tall and skinny, a perfect specimen for worn jeans, cowboy boots and a ten-gallon hat. Francine liked rhinestones, and her preference for glitzy, showy clothing on stage spilled over to her private life. Clover— how she disliked her name!—had a figure like her mother's: curvaceous and totally female.

So she was blond, green-eyed, voluptuous *and* the daughter of two of the most famous country-western performers in the United States. Yet at twenty-six years of age, Clover would gladly trade her looks and bank accounts for a plain mother and father who admitted their affection for each other and didn't give two hoots about fame and fortune.

It would never happen, though, not while either of them had the strength and talent to sing, strum a guitar and draw crowds.

Grimly Clover peered through the rain-washed windshield to the black road ahead, which was just barely revealed by the valiant efforts of her headlights. This was probably a totally wasted trip, she thought again. Francine had succeeded in getting her all worked up about Billy canceling a couple of concerts, but the man certainly had the right to drop out for a few weeks.

Pudge Lang wasn't even alive anymore, although Clover remembered him as an old, old family friend. Why her father should choose to hide out in a place without even a telephone was a mystery.

No, maybe it wasn't a mystery at all. Maybe that's exactly why Billy was at Pudge's old place. Maybe he'd needed to get away by himself for a while.

Or maybe he was sick. Or something.

She *was* worried, Clover admitted to herself, wishing she would see the sign that Francine had told her to watch for. *"It's an itty-bitty sign, Baby, no bigger than a mailbox. Says Lang on it, that's all. You've got to watch real close or you'll miss it."*

Well, she was watching, but all she'd seen for miles and miles was dense forest and rain.

What would Billy say about her just showing up like this? And what if he wasn't even at Pudge's place?

She had more than one worry on her mind, Clover thought with a long-suffering sigh. It would be just like Francine to send her daughter on a wild-goose chase just because she was in an on-again mood about her husband.

Clover squinted as her headlights reflected off of something small and shiny to the right of the road. Yes, she thought with relief. There's the sign. Out of habit, she turned on her right-hand signal light, then shook her head in bemusement. Even a duck would be under cover in this rain, and she hadn't met another car in an hour.

"The house is about a quarter-mile off the highway, Baby, and the road is kind of rough and primitive."

The driveway wound through trees that nearly met overhead. Everything seemed a little eerie, probably because she was driving slowly due to the bad road. She could hear the rain, despite the heavy foliage, and the slaps of the windshield wipers, the purr of the engine. But it still seemed spooky. If she arrived to an empty house on this rainy, black night, she would head back and stop at the nearest telephone to give Francine a piece of her mind— and hope that she woke her up in the bargain!

Clover reached a clearing and spotted the house. She stopped the car to look it over. Its windows were dark, which gave her pause. Billy was a notorious night owl, and if he was here, there should be some lights on.

The house was sort of sprawling. It was wood-sided, brown with white trim. There was another building to the right and just a little behind the house. A garage, probably. At any rate, there was only one vehicle in sight: a battered-looking pickup truck that Clover knew very well didn't belong to her father.

Why did she let Francine talk her into these escapades? Now she had to go up to that strange door and hope to God Billy was inside.

Stepping on the gas ever so lightly, Clover pulled the car closer to the house. She left the headlights on, but turned off the ignition, then grabbed her purse and opened the door before she could scare herself into an attack of pure cowardice.

She ran for the front steps, glad that there was a roof over the small porch. Even so, she got wet, and she gave her shoulder-length hair a shake while she looked for a doorbell. There was only a brass knocker in the middle of the door; she lifted its ring and banged it up and down a few times.

While she waited, she looked around. It was spooky out here all right, as black and silent as a tomb. And wet.

She banged the brass ring against the metal plate again, and this time heard a sound from inside the house. Her heart started jumping. If Billy didn't answer the door, if some stranger stood there, how on earth would she ever explain waking him up at one in the morning?

The porch light came on, nearly blinding her for a second. The door swung open. Clover's heart sank clear to her toes. It wasn't Billy—not even close—who stood there in a pair of unbuttoned, low-slung jeans and nothing else.

What a delicious-looking guy! Tall, wide-shouldered, broad-chested and with a tangle of dark hair right between his lovely pectorals!

Clover took a hasty assessment and rated this sleepy-eyed dream a resounding ten. Lots of black hair, some of it in his eyes, a ruggedly handsome face and a great body. Yes, indeed, definitely a ten.

"Hi," she said with a lot more enthusiasm than she'd arrived with. "Do you know Billy Dove, by any chance?"

"Taking a poll?"

Clover's zest began to fade. "Uh...I was told he was staying here."

"Told by who?"

She could look at this less than enthusiastic reception in several ways. If this guy knew Billy, he could very well be protecting his friend's privacy. On the other hand, Francine might have given her the wrong directions, and this hunk might really be as mean as he sounded.

"I'm Clover Dove, Billy's daughter," she said with a lift of her chin. "Is he here, or am I at the wrong place?"

She watched the guy's eyes move down her body, stop at her toeless sandals for a beat, then move upward again. His gaze paused briefly at strategic points of her figure, then finally lingered on her face. It was the most thorough and uninhibited once-over she had ever received, and she'd received plenty of smoldering looks in her lifetime.

"You don't remember me, do you?" he said then, surprising her.

"Should I?"

"Probably not. Come on in." He stepped back and held the door open.

"Wait a minute! Is Billy here or not?" No way was she going into that house unless her dad was inside, no way! Not after that simmering, inch-by-inch inspection!

"He's here."

"Oh."

"Well, are you coming in or not?"

"Uh...could you wake him up?" She felt about as courageous as a mouse. Maybe Billy was inside and maybe he wasn't. And maybe Mr. Ten was trustworthy and maybe he wasn't.

"You want proof, I take it."

"I don't see his car," Clover said logically.

"It's in the garage."

"Yes, I suppose so." A clever idea occurred to her. "What make is it?"

He shook his head and laughed. "Dizzy dame. Billy's car is a navy-blue Mercedes. Satisfied?"

"I am not a dizzy dame!"

"Don't get all bent out of shape. It's one o'clock in the morning, in case you haven't checked lately. If you want Billy woken up, you do it. I'd rather let him sleep."

Stung and trying not to show it, Clover glanced back to her car. "I left the headlights on, and I have a suitcase."

"I'm barefoot. Do you want me to dress my feet and haul your luggage in for you?"

"Heaven forbid," she drawled. "Sorry I'm such a bother." With that, she whirled around and marched off the porch into the rain. "Arrogant jerk," she muttered as she yanked open the car door, reached in to punch off the headlights and grab the keys. A ten? Hah! More like a minus three! She slammed the door and strode to the trunk. With her suitcase in hand, she marched back to the porch.

The door was still open but the man was gone. A light had been turned on in an inside room, but the foyer was lit only by the porch light. Clover gingerly stepped across the threshold, looked for a light switch and flipped it on when she found one beside the door frame.

She was good and wet. Her white cotton blouse and knee-length split skirt were little protection against the pouring rainfall. Closing the door, she set her suitcase down and thought wryly about great welcomes. Greeting a stranger in the middle of the night might preclude genuine joy on his part, but there was such a thing as simple courtesy.

Then she heard a sound from the room with the light on. Clover followed the sound and light and found herself in a kitchen doorway. The half-dressed man was making a pot of coffee.

"How about showing me to an empty bedroom?" she said sweetly.

"In a minute."

"You're making coffee at one in the morning?"

"I'm awake now, Baby."

Clover's mouth dropped open. "How do you know my nickname? Only Billy and Francine call me Baby."

"And you still call them Billy and Francine. I thought that was really a hoot a few years back."

"How many years back? Do I know you?"

He switched on the automatic drip pot and turned to give her a lopsided grin. "I'm Will Lang."

"Pudge's son? *Billy* Lang?" Ah, yes, little Billy Lang, named after his godfather, Billy Dove. It had been ages since she'd thought about Billy Lang. Smiling, Clover moved farther into the kitchen, folded her arms across her chest and leaned against a cabinet. "Lord, you were a brat!"

Will's grin got wider. "I was an angel alongside you, Baby. Talk about spoiled!"

"I was not spoiled."

"Like hell you weren't! You had every toy ever manufactured and you threw tantrums on an hourly basis. Your mother catered to your whims and your dad jumped when you so much as hinted that he should. I wanted to smack you so bad so many times, my hands itched."

"As I recall, you *did* smack me a few times."

"And got a lacing for it from Pa."

"Pudge, yes." Clover's expression sobered. "I was at the funeral service, you know."

"Yeah, I know. I appreciate it. Sorry if I didn't get around to talking to you. There were hundreds of people, and I missed some of them."

"I didn't see you, either. There was an awfully big crowd. I got there a little late and couldn't sit with Billy and Francine."

"That's probably why I missed you."

"Billy..."

"Will."

She looked him over, seeing again how good-looking he was. Who ever would have thought the rotten little kid she remembered would grow up to look like that? "When did it become 'Will'?"

He smiled. "One 'Billy' in the family is enough."

"Do you see a lot of Billy?"

"More than you do, probably."

Clover stiffened. It wasn't her fault she didn't see a whole lot of her parents. They were always on the go, and she tried to live at least a semblance of a normal existence. "Why did he come here?"

"He comes here a lot. You didn't know that? I think Francine knows."

"She sent me out here." Clover shook her head. "I don't get it. Why was she worried?"

Will shrugged. "Who knows? The coffee's done. Want a cup?"

Clover eyed the pot a moment, then shook her head. "Thanks, but I'm damp clear through and really beat. I think I'll just go to bed. Assuming there's an extra bed in the house."

"Lots of extra beds, Baby."

She gave him a slight frown. "I really wish you wouldn't call me that."

"I remember that you didn't like 'Clover' very much."

"Who could like 'Clover'? It was some ancient ancestor's name on Francine's side of the family. I'll never know why she stuck me with it."

"It's not so bad." Will walked past her. "Where'd you leave your suitcase? Oh, I see it. Come on. I'll show you where you can crash."

Carrying her suitcase, Will led the way down a hallway. He opened the third door they came to, reached into the room and turned on a light. "You can use this room. Bathroom's next door."

Clover went in and looked around. The room was plain but seemed to be clean, and she was tired enough that even a little dirt might not have bothered her. "Thanks."

Will put the suitcase down just inside the door. "Billy didn't know you were coming?"

"I didn't know myself until Francine called me this morning."

"Well, if you hang around until supper tomorrow, I might see you again."

"Oh? You won't be here in the morning?"

Will nodded. "I do cabinet work for a local builder. Good night. Sleep well." The door closed.

Cabinet work? Will Lang held a regular job? Pudge had been Billy's lead guitar man for thirty odd years and must have left his son a pile of money. Why on earth was Will doing that kind of work?

Besides, with his looks he could be anything he wanted to be. Had she ever seen more heavenly blue eyes? Or longer lashes on a man? A better physique? A more electrifying smile?

Shaking her head at her own unusual, practically open-mouthed admiration, Clover lifted her suitcase to the bed and popped its latches open. She dug out the one set of pajamas she'd packed, her robe and slippers and her small cosmetic case.

Yawning, she went to the bathroom next door to get ready for bed.

Two

"Billy!"

"Baby! What in heck are you doing here?"

They met halfway across the kitchen. Billy had been seated at the table, having breakfast in the morning sun and Clover had come trailing in with coffee on her mind. It was almost ten-thirty—she had really slept in.

But apparently so had Billy if he was having breakfast this late.

They hugged enthusiastically, then stood back and checked each another out. "You look beautiful, as always," Billy said.

"And you look...tired. Are you all right?" Clover reached up and touched her dad's face. There were lines there she hadn't noticed before. He was what now...fifty-four? His fabulous platinum hair was losing luster. There was a trace of softness around his waistline, a slight stoop to his bony shoulders.

He was aging, as Francine was, although Clover suspected her mother would go into a permanent decline if anyone hinted at such a thing. Francine was ten years younger than Billy. She had given birth to Clover at eighteen years of age.

"I'm fine," Billy said firmly. "I like to come out here and soak up a little peace and quiet every so often. It's a good place to unwind."

Clover moved to the counter and the coffeepot. "Francine's worried because you canceled some concerts." There was silence behind her, and she turned around.

"Baby... I'm thinking about quitting the business."

"You're ill," she said with her heart in her throat. "You're ill and not telling me!"

"I am not ill! Sometimes you sound just like your mother." Billy returned to his chair at the table and sat down.

"Have you told Francine you might quit?"

"Hell, no! Do you think I want her on my case before I make a decision? And don't you say anything to her, either, understand? She'll know soon enough, one way or the other."

"Then you're still only thinking about it." Clover took her cup of coffee to the table and sat down. The thought of Billy quitting the music business was seeping into her senses. "If you did quit, would you buy a farm, the way you used to say you would someday?"

"Don't know. A farm's a lot of work."

Clover took a sip of coffee. "I could help you."

Billy eyed her across the table. "You'd like that, wouldn't you?"

"I'd love it."

Billy scratched the side of his neck. "You're not a kid anymore, Baby. If you want a farm you should have your own place, with a husband and kids."

Clover rolled her eyes. "Sure, and just where do I find a man who doesn't get all silly and bug-eyed when he learns who my parents are?"

Billy picked up his spoon and ladled up a bite of cereal. "Must be some out there who've got their heads on straight."

"Well, I sure haven't met any. You should see the jerk I went out with last week." Clover set her cup down with a sigh. "I don't know. Sometimes I wonder if I'll ever meet anyone normal."

Billy's pale blue eyes narrowed. "Your mother and I have given you a helluva life, haven't we?"

"Dad, you were always good to me. I always knew you both loved me."

"That's true. We both always loved you, Baby."

Clover smiled. "Last night Will let me in. We talked for a few minutes and he told me I was a spoiled brat when I was a kid. Was I?"

"You?" Billy laughed. "Naw, never. You were perfect, Baby, the sweetest little daughter any man could ever hope for."

Clover picked up her cup with a fond smile. "You don't lie very well, Billy."

He grinned and went back to his cornflakes. "Want some?" he asked, indicating his bowl.

"Later. Billy, how come Will holds down a steady job?"

Billy put his spoon down. "Now, if you want normal, that boy's the most levelheaded person I've ever known. Set your sights on Will Lang, Baby. No woman could do any better. Will's got all kinds of money. But he likes a simple life, so he lives out here, and this sure ain't a mansion, right? He's real good with cabinetry and works for a builder. He'll make some woman a fine husband.''

Clover laughed. ''It doesn't work that way, Billy. A woman can't just set her sights on a guy and make something happen.''

''Why not?''

''You and Francine have the most volatile relationship of any couple I know, and you're suggesting I can *make* something happen with Will Lang? Have you ever been able to make something happen with Francine? Has she with you?''

''You betcha!''

''What?''

''Making sparks is no problem, Baby. Anyone can do that with anyone else, if they want to bad enough. If you're interested in Will, go after him.''

Clover's mouth was hanging open. ''Good grief, who said I was interested? I don't even know Will Lang.''

''Well, *get* to know him!''

''You're something else, Billy. Do you know that?''

''Always have been. Why would I change in my old age?''

They laughed and then fell silent. Billy ate his cereal and Clover drank her coffee. ''How long are you planning to stay out here?'' she asked.

''A while. I don't know.''

''I've got to let Francine know you're all right.''

''You should stay out here for a while, too.'' Billy grinned. ''You could chase Will around the house.''

''Stop that, Billy. Where's the nearest telephone? I've got to call Francine this morning, whatever else happens.''

''Then you'll stay a few days?''

''I didn't bring many clothes.''

Billy grinned again, impishly. "Might do better without 'em."

Clover laughed and shook her head. "I don't believe you said that."

"Just being honest, Baby. I think you're old enough for honesty from your father."

Clover's smile softened. "I think I am. Thanks." She got to her feet. "I'm going to take a shower. Then maybe you'll come with me while I drive to a telephone."

"I don't wanna talk to your mother."

"You don't have to talk to her. Just show me where to go, okay?"

Clover made a credit card call from the pay phone Billy directed her to. "Francine?"

"Baby! Did you find him?"

"He's right where you thought, and he's fine. There's nothing wrong, so you can stop worrying."

"If nothing's wrong, why did he cancel those concerts? Is he there, Baby? Let me talk to him."

Billy was leaning against the hood of her car, and Clover sent her father a pleading look. He blatantly turned his back on her. "I had to drive to a pay phone, Francine. Billy's not with me," she lied.

"Oh. Well, go back to the house and tell him to call me."

"Francine, if he wanted to call you, he wouldn't need me reminding him."

"What's he doing out there in that dreary, godforsaken place? I've seen it. That house is nothing but a hovel."

"It is not a hovel."

"Who else is out there? Is there a woman?"

"A woman! Good Lord, no, there's not a woman. What woman? Who?"

"I've heard a few things. I'm not stupid, Clover, and there are rumors about your father and a young woman named Sara Green."

Clover knew Billy could hear her end of the conversation, and there was suddenly something mighty suspicious about the set of his shoulders. She cleared her throat. "I wouldn't put much stock in rumors, Mother."

"Well, I haven't. If I really believed them, I would have gone out there myself and had it out with your father face-to-face."

"That's why I'm here, then, to see if there's a Sara Green lurking in the vicinity? You might have told me."

"You might not have gone."

"I *definitely* would not have come way out here just to play spy, Francine!"

"Don't be angry, Baby."

"I'm not angry."

"You sound angry."

"Francine, I'm going to stay with Billy for a few days. I'll call you when I get home, okay?"

"Ask Billy to call me."

Clover sighed. "Yes, Mother, I'll ask him to call you."

"I know you're angry."

"I'm not angry. Goodbye, Francine."

Clover hung up and stalked out of the phone booth to the car. She got in without comment, and Billy scurried around to the passenger side and climbed in, also without comment.

Several miles down the road, Clover felt his eyes on her. She looked straight ahead and remained silent.

"Aren't you gonna tell me what got her tail in a wringer?"

"I think you overheard the conversation."

"She's out of shape over Sara Green."

"Do you know a Sara Green?"

"'Course I know a Sara Green! She's a singer. Darned good one, too."

"Francine's heard rumors about you and Sara Green."

"People talk too damned much."

"I'm not asking for any kind of explanation, Billy. But maybe you should call Francine. She'd like to talk to you."

"She's got no intention of talkin', that's the problem. She wants to lay into me, and I'm in no mood to be laid into."

Clover sensed there was something to the rumors, and she bit her lip and frowned. That's why Billy was staying with Will, not to ponder quitting the business, but to avoid a confrontation with Francine about Sara Green.

Clover's heart ached for both of her parents. The divorce rate was high among entertainers. People were drawn to entertainers, married or not, and a long, successful marriage in the music world was something to marvel at.

She pulled the car into the Lang driveway. "I don't think I'll stay, Billy."

He looked at her. "Don't take sides in this, Clover."

"I'm not."

"Sara Green was . . . well, she's a nice girl, but she's not important. Do you get my meaning?"

"I think so."

"Your mother and me…we've had our ups and downs."

"I know." Clover batted her eyelashes to hold back tears. "Call her, Billy."

He shook his head. "Not yet. She's mad and I don't wanna hear it." He smiled suddenly. "There's steaks in the freezer. Let's take 'em out to thaw and plan a fancy dinner for tonight. Surprise Will."

Clover hesitated but finally nodded. She could get only so involved in her parents' seemingly unceasing altercations. "Are you sure Will won't mind my staying?"

Billy opened the car door and got out, with Clover doing the same. "He won't mind. Why would he?"

They trooped into the house. "How come Will doesn't have a telephone?" Clover questioned.

Billy went right to the freezer for the steaks. "He's thinking about putting in a pay phone in the backyard."

"You're kidding."

"He needs a phone once in a while."

"Well, of course he does. But why not have one installed in the house? Billy, that's kind of weird, don't you think?"

"Will ain't weird, just different."

Clover plucked an orange from the fruit bowl. "Pudge was different, too, wasn't he?"

"Yeah, but not in the same way. Pudge was a music man, Will's not. He can play the guitar, though, darned near as good as Pudge did." Billy's expression became nostalgic. "Sure do miss old Pudge."

Clover laid a section of paper towel on the table and sat down to peel her orange as Billy wandered out of the kitchen. In a few minutes she heard the sound of his guitar, the soft, slow strain of a favorite old melody: He was still thinking about Pudge.

Was he really considering quitting the business? Would he ever buy that farm he'd mentioned so many times in the past? Clover sighed. She would chuck everything and move to a farm with her father in a heartbeat, but hanging her hat on that old dream would be pretty foolish.

Because of her parents Clover had hundreds of contacts in the country music world. She sang backup for several important recording stars and did quite a lot of charity work, activities that occupied most of her time. She was invited to nearly every big event in the business, without the pressure of having to attend, so her social life was as busy as she wanted it to be.

But there seemed to be something very meaningful missing in her day-to-day existence. She didn't like thinking that the missing piece was a man—she certainly wasn't a man-hungry female, by any stretch of the imagination—but how else did a woman attain the warmth of home and hearth when that lovely fantasy included children?

Clover had thought of buying a farm by herself a couple of times. At various intervals she had even gone so far as to inspect farms for sale just outside of Nashville. But something always stopped her from proceeding and she'd made no big changes in her life-style.

Perhaps, she thought while eating a section of the orange, it was time to take another look at that option. Wasn't she beyond the age of intertwining her and her parents' futures? As Billy had plainly said, she should have a home of her own.

She did have a home of her own, of course, a very pleasant condo overlooking a pleasing stretch of the Cumberland River. But she knew what Billy had meant. She should go after her own goals.

Gathering up the paper towel and orange peels, Clover got up and discarded them in the trash can under the sink. Three nice steaks were lying on the counter to thaw, which were only the start of a good meal, in her estimation. She went to the refrigerator to see what else was available to round out dinner that evening.

Pulling up near the house around five that afternoon, Will spotted Clover's car and felt a tug of excitement. He'd been hoping all day that she'd still be here. It had been years since he'd seen her and while they hadn't been great pals as kids, they had a lot of shared memories.

The two families had been close when Will and Clover were youngsters. There'd been picnics, fishing trips and weekends of just getting together. But not here. This place had been Pudge's private spot, which he'd bought and used a lot after Will's mother died.

Will liked it. It was off the beaten path and quiet. Billy liked it, too, and showed up for a few days or a week every so often. Francine had been here once, but had made little secret of her negative opinion and never came back. Billy seemed to like the place more because Francine didn't, which both amused and saddened Will, because he cared for Billy Dove in a very special way and only wished the best for his old friend and godfather.

Billy greeted Will at the front door with a tall glass of cold lemonade, which was Will's favorite after-work drink. He had no taste for alcoholic beverages, including beer, although he kept beer in the refrigerator for his friends.

Billy's eyes were sparkling. "Wait till you see what Clover cooked up for supper. That little gal sure knows her way around a kitchen."

Will took the glass of lemonade. "It'll beat my cooking, I bet."

"You're a good cook, but Clover's got an extra-fine touch. How'd your day go?"

"All through with that job now. Got a few days off."

"Hey, that's great. Maybe we should do something."

Will drank half of his lemonade. "Like what?"

"We could go fishing."

"Camp out?"

Billy nodded. "Maybe Clover would go with us."

"You think she would?"

"We'll ask her." Billy went to the kitchen while Will headed down the hall to take a shower. "Will's home."

Clover was putting the finishing touches on a fruit salad for dessert. "I heard."

"The part about the fishing trip, too?"

"Yes."

"Do you wanna go?"

Clover raised her eyes from her task. "I also heard you trying to matchmake by praising my cooking. Since when does putting a couple of salads together and cleaning corn on the cob constitute cooking?"

"You've got corn bread in the oven. That's cooking, ain't it?"

"If Will's impressed with a pan of corn bread, he must be in a bad way."

"Don't be snippy. It ain't becomin'. How about the fishing trip?"

"I don't know. I didn't bring any jeans or anything." Clover was wearing white shorts and a pink T-shirt, and her suitcase contained few other garments, certainly nothing suitable for a fishing and camping outing. Still, it had been ages since she'd gone fishing or spent a night in a sleeping bag, and it really did sound like fun.

"You wanna be coaxed?" Billy teased.

Clover grinned. "You can tell I'd like to go, can't you?"

"It's in your voice, Baby." There was a twinkle in Billy's eyes. "Remember the great times we used to have? You were a darned good little fisherman." He grinned. "I suppose nowadays you have to say fisherwoman, huh? Or fisherperson?"

"Wouldn't surprise me," Clover remarked, giving the fruit salad a final stir. "There, it's all ready."

"Sure is pretty."

They stood there and admired the salad, which was full of strawberries, bananas, pieces of watermelon and some of every other fruit Clover had found in Will Lang's kitchen.

"It's for dessert," Clover said just as Will came in. She couldn't help staring at him. The man was almost too gorgeous to believe.

"What's for dessert?" Will questioned, smiling at Clover with an appreciative expression. If Billy hadn't been present, he might have complimented Clover on her great legs, but that seemed a mite forward in front of a woman's father.

"That there fruit salad," Billy said. "Ain't it something?"

Will's gaze moved to the salad bowl. "Sure is."

Clover said wryly, "It's only a fruit salad, for pete's sake."

"Looks special, though," Billy insisted. "You're just about the most capable little gal I know, Baby. She can do anything she puts her mind to, Will."

Clover sent her father a look of warning. He was going overboard, and if Will didn't catch on as to why Billy was talking so silly, he had to be pretty darned dense. It was embarrassing and Clover said rather sharply, "Check the barbecue grill, Billy. It should be ready for the steaks by now."

Chuckling, Billy went out the back door to the patio. Clover peeked into the oven at the pan of corn bread, and Will helped himself to a strawberry from the salad bowl, commenting, "I sure do like corn bread."

"Don't we all?" Clover returned dryly. She turned from the stove. "Billy asked me to stay for a few days. If you have any objection whatsoever, please don't hesitate to say so. He might forget that this is your home, but I—"

"You're invited to stay for as long as you like."

Their eyes met, and Clover felt a flush starting somewhere in her midsection and radiating outward from there. Something *could* happen between them, if the two of them were together very much.

"Thanks," she finally got out, marveling at the burst of warmth she was feeling.

"You're welcome. Should I take the steaks out to Billy?"

"Uh...yes. Good idea." She practically ran into Will while trying to help him get the platter of steaks. "Sorry." A minute later, when he was outside on the patio with Billy, she ran nervous fingers through her hair. Will Lang was causing some unusual reactions—awkwardness, embarrassment, loss of sensible speech. This wasn't like her, so it had to mean something.

But, in thinking of Will from a personal perspective, he seemed to be a dyed-in-the-wool bachelor and just a tad bit weird. A pay phone in the backyard? Working in construction when he had loads of money? Living way out here all by himself? Billy had labeled Will Lang the most normal guy he knew, but was Billy Dove anyone to judge what was normal?

Hmm, she had better do some serious thinking about those unusual reactions. Certainly she shouldn't just let herself fall into something that she might regret later on.

Three

The meal was tasty, but Billy and Will praised the salads and corn bread until Clover told them point-blank to knock it off. Laughing at her sassy tone, the men started talking about the fishing trip, with their first decision being that it would be an overnight outing. From there the plan evolved into an early departure for the next morning.

They had eaten at the patio table and were still sitting outside. Clover sat back and sipped coffee while she listened. There was a wonderful camaraderie between Will and her father that she enjoyed witnessing. Billy had oodles of friends, but it seemed to Clover that his and Will's friendship was out of the ordinary. She recalled that Billy had sometimes mentioned Pudge's son in the past, and that she had reacted rather disinterestedly, having just barely remembered little Billy Lang.

Her gaze drifted to Will. Other than hair and eye coloring, little Billy Lang wasn't even partially visible in the man across the table. He was her age, maybe a few years older, and a delight to the eye. Clean-shaven, dressed in worn jeans and a white T-shirt, with a smile accompanying most comments, Will Lang was a man few women wouldn't give a second look.

Billy spoke to her. "You are coming with us, aren't you?"

Clover gathered her wandering thoughts. "I really don't have any appropriate clothes with me."

"That's a very small problem," Will said with a glance at his watch. "The stores are still open. We can all drive to town and pick up whatever you need."

"How far is town?" Clover questioned.

"About twenty miles."

Billy stood up. "You two go and I'll do the dishes."

He'd spoken with such commonsense finality that no argument occurred to Clover. She looked to Will for an answer—he might object to the two of them going off alone—and heard from him, "Good plan. Clover?"

Will was agreeable and Billy was all for it, so the decision was hers. Clover got up slowly. "Well . . . I suppose it would be all right. Let me freshen up and change clothes. These shorts—"

"Hey," Billy exclaimed, "there's not much time. You look fine just the way you are. Doesn't she, Will? Don't you think she looks fine just the way she is?"

Will took in her silky blond hair, pink T-shirt, white shorts, long tanned legs and drawled, "She looks fine to me."

Clover's cheeks pinkened. Although Billy had pushed Will into commenting positively on her appearance, she wouldn't be at all comfortable wearing shorts for shopping, whatever either of them might say on the matter. "I'll only be a few minutes."

When she was gone Billy sat down again. "She sure is something, ain't she?"

Will grinned. "Yeah, she sure is, Billy."

"You know," Billy said matter-of-factly, "I wouldn't mind if you and Clover got to be good friends."

"Thanks."

"I mean it, boy. She was complaining just this morning about never meeting a guy who didn't get silly over me and Francine." Billy grinned. "I told her you were as steady as they come."

Will sidestepped the topic. If something happened between him and Clover, fine. If it didn't, that was fine, too. But it wasn't a subject he wished to discuss with her father. "Speaking of Francine, Clover said last night that her mother was the reason she came."

Billy's face fell. "Yeah, Francine sent her out here to check on me. Clover called her this morning and Francine started talkin' about Sara Green."

"Who's Sara Green?"

"An up-and-coming singer. Sara's a nice girl. We got a little too friendly, I guess, and Francine heard about it. It wasn't anything important, Will. There's never been another important woman since the day I met Francine, but road tours get lonely and I guess I spent a little too much time with Sara. Nothing out of line, mind you, but Francine is good at blowing things out of proportion."

"Maybe that's what she heard, Billy. She might not be the one who blew it out of proportion."

"I suppose that could be true," Billy said speculatively.

Will didn't want to offer advice to a man twice his age, but it seemed to him that Billy should clear the air with Francine on the matter of Sara Green. "Rumors can be damned destructive, Billy,'' he said quietly. ''Francine might have good reason to be upset.''

Billy sat silent for a moment, then said, ''We've had a helluva life, Francine and me. Her going one way, me another. It's a wonder we're still married.''

''Success has its price, Billy.''

''It sure does, Will, it sure does.''

Will thought of the similarities between himself and Billy Dove. He wasn't a singer, as Billy was, but he played the guitar well enough to draw attention. After all, he was taught by his father, Pudge Lang, who'd been the best guitar man in the country in his prime. But talent was where the visible similarities stopped. Will had no desire to repeat his father's life, or Billy's. Will followed a second talent, woodworking, and was artistically content to turn out beautiful cabinetry.

There were less obvious likenesses, however, such as their sense of humor, their affection for casual, comfortable clothing, their lack of pretense. Billy was pure country, just as Pudge had been, and so was Will. When it came down to it, Will knew that there probably weren't too many things he wouldn't do for Billy Dove, should Billy ever ask.

There was a question in Will's mind about Clover's preferences. She lived in the city, she *looked* citified, even wearing casual clothing. Her life was music, also, although it was obvious that she wasn't going after stardom. She was pretty enough to make any man sit up and take notice and she had a good personality.

Will was glad Clover had come and glad that she was going camping with him and Billy. For that matter, he was just a little bit schoolboy thrilled about the shopping expedition. It wasn't a date, but he welcomed the opportunity to get to know her better.

Clover returned, wearing white slacks in place of the shorts. Her hair was brushed and there was evidence of cosmetics on her face. Will smiled: She looked great.

He and Billy got to their feet. "The stores close at nine," Will said, "so we should be back before ten, Billy. You can dig out the sleeping bags and camping gear, if you want to. Everything's in the storage room behind the garage."

"I'll get it all ready."

"What about food?" Clover asked.

"I know what to pack," Billy said. "Go along now and get your shopping done. And don't hurry back on my account."

Clover didn't know whether to laugh or cry over her father's transparency. She glanced at Will and saw understanding in his eyes, which made her feel better. At least he wasn't being completely taken in by Billy's efforts to play matchmaker.

There was a short debate on which vehicle to use, but in the end they took Clover's car, and Will drove.

Once on the road, Clover commented, "On the way back I'd like to stop and make a few phone calls." She gave Will a questioning look. "It's none of my business, I know, but why don't you have a telephone?"

"Pa never put one in and I've made very few changes in the place."

"But it's so inconvenient."

"I don't make many calls."

"Billy said you were thinking about putting a pay phone in the backyard."

Will laughed. "I think he likes that idea. I mentioned it one time and he never forgot it."

"He'd see the humor in it, all right," Clover replied. "But the phone company really wouldn't put a pay phone in someone's backyard, would it?"

"I never investigated. I'd probably have to buy one." Will sent Clover a smile. "I should go ahead and do it, just to see Billy's face."

Clover laughed. "He'd love it, I'm sure."

Will glanced at her again. "Too bad we got so far out of touch, Baby."

"Clover, please."

"None of your friends call you Baby?"

"Only Billy and Francine."

"Are you involved with anyone?"

The question didn't surprise Clover. In fact, it seemed perfectly natural and she didn't hesitate to answer. "No, I'm not. Are you?"

"No."

Questions flitted through Clover's mind, personal questions about the women in his past. How many? Who were they? Had there ever been one who'd been really important?

"You've never been married?" she asked.

"No, never. Have you?"

"Not even close." Clover suspected that Will Lang might fall over with shock if he ever found out that she was still a virgin. So would everyone else she knew, for that matter. That information was a well-guarded secret, something she wouldn't relate to even her closest girlfriends. When any of them talked about men, she pretended to know everything they did, and most of them knew plenty, whether they were married or not. It always amazed Clover that women she knew very well, and liked a great deal, could have such a breezy attitude about something that seemed so crucial to a relationship.

Her own attitude was very outdated, she'd come to realize, and it was because of the ethics and standards passed on to her from Francine and Billy. Despite a seemingly free and easy life-style, her parents advocated a rather strict morality.

Which was why their present problem—Sara Green—was so unsettling.

When they reached the town of River Oaks, Will asked her what she wanted to buy.

"Jeans, primarily," Clover responded. "A pair of sneakers, some socks, things like that."

"Then Burton's should do it." Will drove a few blocks and pulled into the parking lot of a sizable store.

Inside, Will followed her around the women's department for a few minutes, then wandered off. It didn't take Clover long to buy two pairs of jeans, a pair of sneakers, socks and a lightweight jacket, because she took what the store had without worrying about price or style. With her purchases, she went looking for Will and found him in the sporting goods section.

He was looking at lanterns and gave Clover a surprised smile. "Done already?"

"All through. Do you need a new lantern?"

"This one looks good, don't you think?" He held it up.

"Looks good to me, but I'm no expert on lanterns."

"It's supposed to give off a special light that won't attract insects."

"Any light attracts insects."

"Think I'll buy it. Maybe it'll work." Will carried the lantern up to the cashier. The woman seemed distracted and when she made a mistake in the change she gave Will, he corrected her. "You gave me ten dollars too much, ma'am."

Clover was standing by, watching. "I did?" the woman said, sounding as though she thought him wrong.

"Yes." Will counted the bills in his hand. "See? Ten dollars too much." He held the ten out with a grin. "You'll need this to balance your register tonight."

Belief altered the woman's expression. "Why, you're right! Thanks a lot. I'd have looked for that ten for a long time."

"You're welcome."

On the way out of the store, Clover commented on the incident. "You're a nice guy, Will Lang. Honest."

"Do you like nice guys, Clover Dove?"

"I'm not sure I've known very many."

They stopped at the car and Will opened the trunk for their packages. He closed the lid and turned to Clover. It was nearly dark and the parking lot's lights were on. "Maybe we should get to know each other," he said softly.

She returned his admiring, unblinking gaze. "Maybe we should."

"You're beautiful, Baby. Seriously beautiful. I wanted to say that all through dinner." Will smiled. "And you make great corn bread."

Clover laughed and whacked him on the arm. "Mention that corn bread again and you die, Billy Lang." Her expression softened. "But thanks for the compliment. I think you really mean it."

"Count on it. Now, let's go home and get ready for that camping trip. I've got a feeling that it's going to be something special."

Will stopped at the pay phone so Clover could make her calls. The first one was to Francine. "We're going camping, Billy, Will Lang and me. We're planning to do some fishing."

"You are?"

Was it her imagination or was there a trace of longing in her mother's voice? "Anyway, I wanted you to know that I'll be out of touch for a few days."

"Billy didn't call, Baby."

"I asked him to."

"Where are you going camping?"

"They talked about Bear Creek."

"Good choice. You'll have fun. It's been a long time since you saw Will. What do you think of him?"

"He's pretty nice, Francine."

"He was really good-looking the last time I saw him."

"He still is."

"You sound interested."

"I might be. He's waiting in the car, Francine, and I have another call to make. I'll call again when we get back from Bear Creek."

"Say hello to your father for me. You might mention again that I'd like to hear from him."

"I will, Mother. Bye."

"Just a second! Tell Billy...oh, blast it, tell him I'm sorry! I never should have listened to that stupid gossip about him and Sara Green. Tell him that, Baby."

"Gladly, Mother. Bye."

Clover's second call was to John Domaney, the rehearsal director for the video she was singing backup on. Not positive she would connect with John, Clover was relieved to reach him. The conversation was brief, since Clover merely wanted to make sure that her extended absence wouldn't conflict with John's schedule. He assured her that she wouldn't be needed for another week, and the call put an end to any concern Clover had on the matter.

She returned to the car. "Everything okay?" Will asked as she got in.

Clover wondered if Will had ever met Sara Green, but she couldn't discuss Billy's and Francine's problems, not with anyone. "Everything's fine."

During the short drive to the house, Will brought up a topic he'd been wondering about. "Do you like living in Nashville?"

"It's home," Clover replied, then sighed. "I like city life well enough, but my dream's always been of living on a farm."

Surprised, Will raised an eyebrow. "Ever lived on one?"

"No, but they always look so pretty driving by. Everything's so green and neat."

"Not all farms are green and neat. Takes hard work to keep 'em that way."

"I might have sounded a bit childish, Will, but I fully understand that a well-kept farm takes work."

"I didn't mean to patronize you, or make fun of your dream. We'd be a pretty sorry lot without dreams, Baby."

Clover turned in the seat to look at him. "Are you going to continue calling me that?"

Will took his eyes off the road to meet hers. This lady was really getting to him. "It fits you, honey," he said softly.

A shiver went up Clover's spine. Will was a sexy, handsome guy, and he was becoming more deeply embedded in her system with each passing minute. Knowing that fact created an exciting feeling, one that was brand-new and quite delicious to savor.

Still, she shouldn't get too eager about a man with Will's life-style, although that, too, had some appeal. But what did she really know about Will Lang? Maybe he had a slew of girlfriends. Maybe he could say pretty things to her so easily because he was well practiced.

Clover faced front. Pretending to know things about men and sex with her female friends was a far cry from actual experience. Will Lang wasn't a virgin, she'd be willing to bet.

"I still wish you'd call me Clover," she said quietly.

Will nodded. "All right, I will." After a moment, he added, "Unless we're alone. I can't guarantee what I might call you when we're alone."

Another shiver struck Clover's spine. There was intimacy in Will's voice, and she didn't have to be experienced to know that he was hinting at a lot more than conversation between them in that last remark.

Will stopped Clover's car in his yard where it had been parked before. When he turned off the headlights and ignition, everything was suddenly very dark. She felt him leaning toward her and then his hand sliding around her shoulders, urging her forward.

She let it happen, let him draw her close enough for a kiss. His mouth moved over her face, slowly, and she barely breathed until it found her lips. A lovely weakness invaded her body at the contact, and she knew after a moment that Will would prolong the kiss as long as she allowed it.

Breathless, she turned her face away. "We'd better go in."

His hand squeezed her shoulder. "You're very nice to kiss."

Clover didn't know how to respond to such a comment, so she said nothing and fumbled around in the dark for the door handle. Will's door opened first, and the overhead light came on. Clover quickly got out.

They unloaded the trunk and carried everything around to the back of the house, where Billy was happily stacking gear on the patio for the camping trip.

"Get everything you need?" he asked his daughter.

"Everything," Clover confirmed. "Listen, are we taking suitcases, or what?" She eyed the pile of camping and fishing gear. "This looks like an awful lot of stuff."

"This is going to be a first-class camping trip," Billy stated proudly.

Will grinned. Billy had dug out nearly every piece of camping equipment Will owned, and the storage room had contained a lot. "You can take your suitcase or put your things in a canvas bag, Clover, whichever you prefer."

"How are we going to haul everything?" she questioned.

"Will's pickup," Billy stated.

Clover had been avoiding Will's eyes, but she finally looked at them and felt an instantaneous jolt. Their deep blue depths contained a message, one that stated quite clearly that things had only just begun for her and Will.

Uncertain about her participation in that scenario, Clover hurried into the house. The kitchen was clean; Billy really had done the dishes. She passed through the room and went down the hall to her bedroom, where she dropped her packages on the bed.

Will's kiss was still on her mouth, and she placed her fingertips to her lips and frowned. Worrying about camping with Will for two days was silly, she told herself. Billy would be there, certainly preventing any serious hanky-panky. And the kiss had been sweetly undemanding, nothing to get defensive about.

After her new things were tucked into her suitcase, Clover wandered out to the patio, where Will and Billy were hauling camping equipment to the pickup. Clover caught Billy's arm during one of Will's trips.

"I called Francine again." Billy didn't look pleased. "I had to tell her I was going to be out of touch, Billy. Anyway, she said to tell you she's sorry that she listened to those rumors about Sara Green.''

"She did? She really said she's sorry?''

"Her words exactly.''

"She didn't sound mad anymore?''

"No, she didn't.''

"Hmm. Maybe I'd better give her a call.''

Clover smiled. "That would be nice.''

"I'll do it right now. Will,'' he called, starting for the garage and his Mercedes. "I'm going down to the pay phone to call Francine.''

Will's voice came back to the patio. "Go right ahead, Billy. I'll get the rest of this stuff loaded.''

Clover picked up a sleeping bag and brought it to the pickup. She handed it up to Will, who was on the bed of the truck arranging things in some kind of order.

"Thanks,'' he said with a smile. "But you don't have to help.''

"I want to.''

"Don't lift anything heavy.''

Smiling, Clover went back to the patio for another load. By the time Billy's Mercedes drove into the yard, the pickup was all packed. Even most of the food, everything but the items that needed to stay cold, had been brought out and stowed on the truck bed. In the morning, they could bring out their clothes and the ice chests, and they'd be ready to leave in no time.

Clover's excitement had been mounting. Two days at Bear Creek with Billy and Will were going to be a rare treat. Will had talked about pan-fried trout and made her mouth water, and she knew that Billy would take his guitar and there'd be music around the camp fire. She'd put in a package of marshmallows for roasting, and could almost taste their smoky, syrupy flavor.

Billy left his car in the yard, rather than returning it to the garage, which gave Clover a funny feeling. She waited at the back of the pickup with Will for Billy to get out and walk over to them.

"Looks like you got everything all done," Billy remarked.

"What's wrong?" Clover asked.

Billy cleared his throat. "Uh...kids...I don't think I can go with you."

Clover's heart sank. "Why not? Billy, we're all packed."

"I know, I know." Billy rubbed his mouth. "It's like this, Baby. Your mother wants me to come home for a few days. Things haven't been so good between us...you understand...and, well, how could I refuse?"

Words escaped Clover. She couldn't even say how disappointed she was, not when her parents were speaking to each other again. But she was disappointed, so much so that she felt like bawling. She felt Will come up behind her. "You and I can go, Clover."

She turned and gave him an incredulous look. "Alone?"

Billy eagerly chimed in. "Sure you can, honey. You two are old friends. There's nothing wrong with old friends taking a fishin' trip together."

"Will and I are not old friends, Billy," she pointed out. "We knew each other as kids, but—"

"Clover," Will interrupted in a soothing tone. "There are two tents on the truck. Billy and I were going to share the big one, but you can use it and I'll take the smaller one."

"No sense in canceling the trip just 'cause I can't go," Billy said in such a logical manner, Clover felt like smacking him. She should go, she thought. She should go and give Will Lang every freedom. It would serve Billy right if...if she came back pregnant!

Both men were looking at her, hopeful, and she was doing her best to appear adult and nonplussed, when she still felt like crying. The truck was loaded, she'd bought new jeans and sneakers, she'd planned on eating pan-fried trout and roasted marshmallows—she'd wanted to go, dammit!

She still did.

Her gaze settled on her father. "When are you leaving?"

"Uh . . . just as soon as I get my stuff together."

"Tonight, then." She glanced at Will and saw her own thoughts on his face: if she stayed, they'd be alone for two days and nights.

Will shifted his weight from one foot to the other. There were things he could say to reassure Clover, but he felt pretty awkward with Billy standing there. It seemed, in the very next moment, that Billy caught on, because he began backing away.

"I guess you two will have to decide," he said. "Don't be mad at me, Baby."

"I'm not mad at anyone," Clover sighed.

Will turned and shuffled something around in the pickup bed until Billy was inside the house. Then he leaned against the truck and looked at Clover. "Are you worried about that kiss?"

She lifted her chin. "Should I be?"

Nothing was said for a moment, then Will pushed away from the truck. "I can't promise not to want to kiss you again, but you can always say no."

Can I rely on that? she wondered. A trifle addled over the unexpected turn of events, Clover shook her head. "Guess I'll go in and see if Billy needs any help."

"Clover," Will said as she walked away.

She stopped. "What?"

"Are you going to be here in the morning to go camping with me?"

She raised her eyes to the heavens and admired the stars, then finally answered. "Yes, Will, I'm going to be here in the morning to go camping with you."

He smiled as she headed for the house.

Four

A loud pounding woke Clover. Peeking through eyelids that wouldn't quite open, she groaned. The room was still dark and someone was trying to knock down her door. "Go away," she mumbled and pulled the covers over her head.

"Clover? If you're going with us, get on the bus!" a voice rumbled cheerily through the closed door.

"Who's 'us'?" she grumbled.

"Merely a figure of speech," Will called. "I'm the only one here. Do you need some help getting out of bed?"

Muttering to herself, Clover pushed the blankets away from her face. "It's still pitch-black!"

"It's 4:00 a.m. Rise and shine!"

"Oh, Lord," she moaned and then indulged in a yawn so enormous, it stretched the corners of her mouth.

"Clover?"

"I'm up!" she yelled grouchily. "Go away so I can take a shower." A shower would clear her sleep-fogged brain. Why in heaven's name should a camping trip start at 4:00 a.m.?

Will chuckled. "The coffeepot's on."

"Good," Clover mumbled, untangling herself from the sheets to put her feet on the floor. She sat there for a minute to get her bearings, then pushed herself up. Yawning again, she located her cosmetic case and clothes.

When she walked into the kitchen twenty minutes later, Will handed her a mug of coffee. She managed a relatively normal, "Thanks."

"It's going to be a nice day. Not a cloud in sight," Will commented, then peered at her. "Everything okay?"

Clover took a sip of coffee. "I'm not sure. I don't remember your saying anything about leaving in the middle of the night."

Will folded his arms. "Not much of a morning person, huh?"

"An understatement," Clover replied dryly, and took another swallow of coffee.

"Early morning's the best part of the day."

"Possibly. It's really not a point I can debate, not having had much experience with starting the day even before the proverbial early bird."

"Have to teach you some better habits," Will said with an amused glint in his eyes.

Clover was finally coming awake. The shower had helped but the hot, strong coffee was helping more. She looked around the kitchen and noted that the ice chests were missing. "You must have already loaded the cold food."

"Everything's ready to go." Will grinned. "Everything but you."

"I'm ready."

"I thought we'd catch breakfast on the road some-where."

"Fine with me. I couldn't eat anything now anyway."

"Is your suitcase all set to go?"

Clover set down her mug. "I'll get it."

"Go ahead and drink your coffee. I'll take care of it."

"Thanks," Clover mumbled as Will walked away. How could anyone look so fresh and be so cheerful at four in the morning? Of course, she'd had a little trouble falling asleep last night and Will had probably conked out the minute his head hit the pillow. For some silly reason, she'd laid there and thought about the two of them being alone in the house. And then about them being alone at Bear Creek for another night. At one point she'd considered hanging her father by his thumbs for putting her in such an uncomfortable situation, but getting down to hard facts, no one had forced her to agree to anything. When Billy left, she could have gone, too.

Will passed through the kitchen with her suitcase, carrying it outside to the pickup. After a minute, Clover heard three short toots of his horn. Apparently the man was eager to get started. Sighing, she went to the back door and called, "Do you want the lights turned out?"

"They're all out except for the kitchen light. Leave that one on," Will called back. "Just close the door behind you. It'll lock on its own."

On the way from the house to the truck, Clover took a look at the sky. The stars were fading, and dawn was a long thin line of silvery light on the eastern horizon. The air was cool and damp, and suddenly she felt alive and wide-awake.

Will had the truck's engine running. Clover climbed up into the passenger seat and settled in. While Will turned the pickup around and started down the crude road through the trees, Clover took a good look at him. There was enough light to see him quite clearly, and it struck her as incongruous that she and Will Lang were together at all, let alone heading out for a camping expedition.

She sighed. He was gorgeous, even at five in the morning, wearing a black-and-white plaid shirt, jeans, boots and a black leather belt with a silver buckle. Something white protruded from his shirt pocket, an envelope maybe.

Will sent her a smile. "Haven't been camping in quite a spell."

"How come?"

"No particular reason. Just didn't get around to it, I guess."

"I can't even remember the last time I went camping. No, wait, I think Billy took me camping when I was about thirteen. We went to Kiley's Point. Yes, that's right, Kiley's Point."

"Would you rather go there than Bear Creek? We could, if you'd like. It's not much farther."

Clover shrugged. "Makes no difference. I like both places. Which one has the best fishing?"

"Bear Creek, if you want trout. There's good bass at Kiley's Point, but Bear Creek's got the trout."

"Let's stay with Bear Creek," Clover said positively. "I've been thinking a lot about pan-fried trout."

"That was Dad's favorite fishing spot."

"Ah, yes," Clover murmured. "Pudge was something else, wasn't he? You must miss him terribly."

"I do," Will said. "We were close. Like you and Billy. Too bad Billy couldn't come with us."

"Yes, too bad," Clover agreed quietly, hoping in her heart that Billy and Francine had made up and that peace would reign in the Dove family for a while.

"You know something else that's too bad?" Will said. "You and I losing touch. I thought about that again last night after we went to bed."

Clover sent him a sharp glance. So, while she was lying in bed thinking about him, he was doing the same about her. Knowing that gave her an odd feeling, one that contained a good amount of warmth. Liking Will Lang was maybe the easiest thing she'd ever done, and maybe it was all right. Maybe something very nice was happening to them.

They settled into relaxed conversation. While Will drove, he told her about making cabinets, and Clover responded with stories about her life in Nashville. They didn't function on precisely common ground, but neither were their routines incompatible.

The sun came up bright and hot. Around seven Will pulled into a roadside café, and they ate a hearty breakfast of pancakes and country sausage. When they were back in the pickup and on the highway, Will took the envelope from his shirt pocket and held it out to her. "Brought you something."

Clover took the envelope curiously. "What is it?"

"Some old snapshots. Take a look."

Inside the envelope were a handful of photos, taken when she and Will were kids. Smiling nostalgically, Clover sat back to study them. Billy and Francine were in one shot with her, all three of them much younger and laughing. There was one of Billy, Pudge and Will. Several had been taken at a birthday party.

"These are wonderful," Clover murmured. "I haven't seen them before."

"They were in Pa's things. I dug them out last night. Thought you might get a kick out of seeing them."

Clover continued to examine the pictures. Were there old snaps of Will in the Dove family albums? He'd been a handsome boy, although the devil himself was on little Billy Lang's face in these shots.

Clover began laughing. "Do you remember what you did at this party?"

Will grinned. "What'd I do?"

"Put a cricket in my cup of lemonade."

"Nah," Will said with exaggerated disbelief. "I wouldn't do something like that."

"You were full of mischief, Will Lang, and you not only put a cricket in my lemonade, but you also tried to put one down the neck of my dress."

"And you screamed three octaves above middle C. Lord, you could scream!" Will chuckled. "I think I purposely did things to make you scream. Used to drive our folks nuts."

"And you called *me* a brat the other night," Clover retorted.

"And spoiled," Will reminded.

"I was no more spoiled than you were, and you know it."

"Guess we were both spoiled, huh?"

Clover smiled. "Guess we were."

They arrived at Bear Creek by midmorning. "Hey, we're in luck," Will exclaimed as he parked the pickup beneath a massive oak tree. "There's no one else here."

The spot was beautiful. Mammoth old trees, clean air sparkling with sunshine and the creek, about ten feet wide and burbling over rocks in its path, creating a special kind of music. They walked around the clearing. "We'll put the tents over there," Will said, indicating a grassy area with a well-established fire pit.

Clover's gaze went to the treetops, which were a rich green against the vivid blue sky. "This is great, Will."

"Sure is." Will went back to the pickup and opened the tailgate. Clover reached for a box. "Don't lift anything heavy," he cautioned, just as he'd done last night, which brought a smile to Clover's lips.

"What do you think I am, Lang, some kind of panty-waist?" Clover took the box. "Where do you want this stuff set down?"

"Near the fire pit. We'll stack it all together and sort it out later. As soon as the truck's unloaded, I'll put up the tents."

It took about a dozen trips for each of them to transport everything on the pickup bed to the grass near the fire pit. Clothes, food, tents, bedding, camp stove, utensils—certainly enough stuff to stay out there for a week. On the next-to-last trip, when Clover and Will were heading back to the truck, he casually dropped his arm around her shoulders.

"You're okay, kid," he complimented lightly.

"Because I helped you unload?" Clover noticed her faster heartbeat, just because Will's arm was loosely draped around her. She looked up into his blue, blue eyes and experienced a melting sensation.

At the back of the pickup, they stopped. Will put his hands on her waist and smiled. "You're okay for a lot of reasons, Baby," he said softly.

She could feel the heat of his big hands on her waist, and from her many reactions she knew that Will Lang was seeping deeper and deeper into her system. It was okay. Her last date, which she'd been roped into by friends, had been with a rock guitarist who'd worn purple-and-white zebra-striped sack pants, gold boots and an earring. Will was as normal as they came—no earrings, no zebra stripes.

And he wasn't even remotely interested in the music business. A cabinetmaker. How marvelous.

They stood there and looked at each other, both wearing a hint of a smile. There wasn't only affection between them, there was also gladness, joy.

Clover would not refuse a kiss, Will suspected. And he considered kissing her for a long, lovely moment.

But he decided they had best stick to camping, at least for a while. "I'd better get those tents set up," he said, and let her go.

Some magical instrument was strumming a lilting song in Clover's soul as she watched Will pull the last items from the truck bed. She liked the way he moved, the way his thick, glossy hair shaped to his head, the breadth of his shoulders, his long legs and slender hips.

She wondered again, in the next breath, about the women Will knew. A man who looked as he did couldn't possibly be totally unattached. Somewhere in his life, within his usual routines, there had to be women. Or worse, *one* woman. Someone special.

But if there was, would he be letting Clover know that he liked her? Somehow she didn't think so. Will struck her as sincere by nature, a genuinely nice guy.

Clover tried to help with the job of setting up the tents, but Will was so sure of what he was doing—and she knew so little about the process—she mostly stood by and chatted with him while he worked.

They talked about nothing important, about some bees buzzing among a patch of dandelions, about a bright red cardinal that appeared for a few moments then flew away, about the temperature, which seemed to be climbing to the high eighties.

It was very pleasant. Will was easy to talk to. Clover could be herself and say whatever came to mind, about bees and birds, that is. When she reversed that phrase and thought about "the birds and the bees," she became slightly flustered. But that was really what was uppermost in her mind—Will Lang's indisputable sex appeal.

Never, she had to admit, had she looked at a man in quite the same way that she was looking at Will. Oh, she'd wondered about sex with certain men, any normal woman did. But desire had not been present during those few and far between moments of carnal speculation. Not her own, at any rate, and just watching Will move around made her feel rather feverish.

He organized the camp quickly and efficiently. Clover put her suitcase in the largest tent, and with Will's instructions, made up a comfortable bed consisting of an air mattress, a thick pad and a soft, cushy sleeping bag.

Finally everything was neat and exactly where Will wanted it. He put his hands on his hips. "Are you hungry?"

"No, are you?"

"Not a bit. Let's go fishing."

While Will laid out the fishing gear, Clover went into her tent and dropped the flap. The jeans and top she'd put on that morning were becoming much too warm. She emerged a few minutes later wearing white shorts and a sleeveless blouse.

Will took one look at all that bare skin and tossed her a can of insect repellent. "You'd better spray some of this on yourself."

"Oh! Maybe I shouldn't have changed."

He grinned. "Don't change back. I like the view."

Laughing, Clover applied the insect repellent to her legs and arms. "Don't they make this stuff with a better smell?" she questioned, wrinkling her nose.

"If people liked it, maybe bugs would like it, too, which would sort of defeat its purpose." Will moved closer to her. "Got a hat? And you need some sunscreen for your face." His gaze traveled her features. "Damn, you're pretty. How am I supposed to concentrate on catching trout with such a pretty woman in plain sight?"

"By the time I get gooped up with insect repellent and sunscreen, you won't have a problem, Lang," Clover drawled, although Will's teasing flattery made her chest feel tight.

"You look great in shorts. Best legs I've ever seen."

Clover cleared her throat. From the expression on Will's face, she suspected that he had a few ideas beyond catching trout. Whatever was developing between them was exciting, but she didn't want them moving too fast. "Are we going fishing or are we going to stand around here admiring limbs and such?"

"Not just any limbs," Will pointed out with a sassy grin.

"Be that as it may, Mr. Lang, the trout are waiting." Clover took a step away from him. "Which pole will I be using?"

She wasn't playing coy and hard to get, Will realized with a broader grin. He sensed no wall between them, merely a little common sense. "The gray and silver one," he replied, picking up the rod and reel and handing it to her. "Know how to use a fly rod?"

"It's been a while, but I think I can manage."

"Let's see your technique."

Clover raised the rod, held the line with her left hand the way she remembered and whipped the pole a few times. "How's this?"

"Not bad. Get your hat and let's go."

* * *

They caught five nice trout. Will cleaned the fish and buried the debris away from camp, while Clover cleaned herself with a basin of water inside her tent. The insect repellent was so vile-smelling that she decided to brave the mosquitoes and gnats without it. After a good wash, she put on the jeans again, fixed her hair and used a few cosmetics.

They were planning to eat lunch and then take a hike, which was why Clover had opted for the jeans. She was in a fantastic mood, with laughter lurking in her system and her head just a bit in the clouds. Will was fun. He'd laughed uproariously when she got her line snagged in a tree, then patiently helped her untangle it. He'd teased her initial efforts to place the colorful fly on the end of her line exactly where she wanted it in the water, and then gave her a lesson in wrist-flicking.

"It's all in the wrist, honey. Flick it, like this."

"You 'flick' marvelously well," she'd told him with a straight face.

He'd grinned smugly. "Yeah, I do, don't I?"

He did everything well, she thought, from setting up camp to cleaning fish to flicking a fishing line.

She liked him, more than she'd ever liked anyone. He was sweet and funny and so handsome she felt a rolling sensation in her belly every time she looked at him.

"Hey," Will said on the other side of her tent flap. "Gonna stay in there all day?"

"Nope!" Smiling, Clover lifted the flap and stepped out. "I'm clean and shiny and—"

"Beautiful," Will finished softly, with his gaze washing over her. He grinned. "Wait until you taste those trout tonight. You'll probably beg me to marry you, just so I can cook trout for you on a regular basis."

He was teasing, of course, but Clover felt her cheeks heating up. "Maybe I'll just hire you," she returned pertly. "Marrying someone just to get a trout expert would be a bit impulsive."

"Yeah, but maybe I'm also an expert in other areas, and think what you might be missing by merely putting me on the payroll." Will grinned and walked off to where he'd set up the folding table and chairs.

Clover didn't have to ask to which "areas" Will might be referring. Obviously he was hinting at kissing and more, and she wasn't sure how to respond. If she pooh-poohed his bragging, he just might offer to give her an example of his expertise, which was both exciting and a trifle daunting to contemplate.

At any rate, there was food on the table, bread, cold meat and condiments for sandwiches. There was also a plastic container with the remains of last night's fruit salad and frosty cans of soda and lemonade. They sat down to eat.

"Clover Dove," Will said softly, looking at her across the small table. "Baby Dove."

She grimaced. "Sounds like an infant bird."

"Yeah, it does. But that's not what I think of when I say it and look at you, though."

"I'm not going to ask what you're thinking, Will Lang, so stop hinting."

"That's because you already know what I'm thinking."

"*Stop* thinking and eat your lunch," Clover retorted.

"Then I can't even ask where you've been all my life."

"It's a corny line, anyway. I'd be disappointed if you used it."

"You don't like 'lines,' huh?"

"What I don't like is phoniness, and there's nothing phonier than the dumb lines some guys lay on women."

They ate in silence for a few minutes. Then Will said, "I've been thinking about getting a motor home. Ever traveled in a motor home?"

"Billy had one for a while. Didn't you ever see it?"

"Oh, yeah, that's right. About five years ago, wasn't it?"

"About that."

"How come he got rid of it? Didn't he like it?"

"He liked it, but Francine didn't. Billy would load it up with friends and take off for a weekend somewhere. Mother was sure he was going to kill half of Nashville in one fell swoop. She maintained that he didn't know how to drive it, especially when he and his friends got to partying."

"A motor home is no more dangerous to drive than anything else, but partying and driving don't mix in any vehicle," Will said.

"True. Anyway, Billy sold the motor home. I took one jaunt with him, and I thought it was pretty neat. It had everything—a kitchen, a bathroom, even a satellite dish."

"A luxury model."

"Definitely."

Will grinned. "If I bought one, would you take a jaunt with me?"

Clover moistened her suddenly dry lips with a sip of soda. Luxury model or not, that motor home had been very close quarters. "Depends."

"On what, Clover?"

Will wasn't grinning anymore. His eyes were urging honesty and they contained an extremely personal light. A thundering awareness shook Clover: She could fall awfully hard for Will Lang, and if this camping trip didn't do it, a jaunt in a motor home together certainly would.

She didn't want to be serious with Will yet, and that's what he was asking for. Deliberately she shaped a teasing smile. "It depends on how good those trout are tonight."

Her ploy worked. Will relaxed and laughed. "If that's your measure, you'll probably go around the world with me and my motor home."

"That good, huh?" Clover said skeptically.

"Better than that. You'll probably do anything I suggest after you taste my trout."

Clover smiled sweetly. "Just don't suggest anything I wouldn't do under any circumstances, Will Lang."

He cocked an eyebrow. "Interesting comment, Clover Dove. Very interesting."

Five

The hike, supposedly an innocuous activity, turned out to be the most sensually provoking event of Clover's life. They went upstream of Bear Creek, following a trail that wasn't always clearly defined. They walked single file in places, ducking brush and tree branches, and abreast in others, enjoying unrestricted sunlight. Sometimes Will took Clover's hand. Once, climbing over some boulders, he helped her hop down from one by grasping her waist.

Throughout, even when they weren't in direct contact, Clover felt Will's tug, his pull. His eyes looked to be brimming with secrets, his smiles thrilled her. She kept glancing at his mouth and remembering his kiss.

And he wasn't teasing, as he'd done while they fished. Instead, he pointed out trees—hawthorns, oaks, hackberries; birds—a purple martin, some swallows and meadowlarks; even weeds and wild geraniums and several different species of clover.

She was impressed with his knowledge of the outdoors. Tennessee forests were beautiful and lush, and while she recognized much of the growth and birds Will showed her, she hadn't known them all by name.

Regardless, Clover suspected the conversation about plants and birds was merely to cover some awkwardness. It was possible that Will had other things on his mind, but without a sign from her, he wouldn't say them.

As they trudged along, Clover thought about it. Was she ready to give Will Lang a subtle signal? She would like him to kiss her again, and she would like to kiss him. But they were a long way from home and very alone. Was it wise to start something she wasn't completely sure of?

And she always came back to their short acquaintance-ship, never mind their childhood interaction. They hadn't seen each other in years, and maybe Will was a good friend of Billy's, but she didn't know him all that well.

Then, out of the blue, her thoughts would reverse. When had she liked anyone more? When had she laughed so easily with a man? Enjoyed his teasing and teasing him back?

If Billy had come with them, as planned, there would not be so much tension developing between her and Will. And there was still the evening and night to get through.

Will was walking fast. "Wait," Clover breathed, and sat on a large rock. "I'm getting tired."

He turned and came back. "Sorry."

"I'm not used to hiking so far. You must be in great shape." Clover couldn't look at him after that comment. There was no question, after all, about Will Lang's physical perfection.

Will hunkered down beside the rock. "Maybe you need to get more exercise than you're getting."

"Undoubtedly."

He grinned. "After you eat my trout and beg me to marry you and I fight you off for a few weeks and finally succumb, I'll see to it that you get lots of exercise."

He was teasing again, but Clover got the feeling that the exercise he had in mind wasn't hiking through the woods.

"Maybe I'll eat your trout and hate it so much that I'll start a movement to have you banished from Tennessee," she returned in the same bantering tone he'd used.

"But then you wouldn't get that exercise." Will laid a hand on her knee. "Getting your wind back?"

Their eyes met, and Clover's breath caught in her throat. He had switched from teasing to serious in the blink of an eye. "I was."

"You make me breathless, too, Baby."

"Will . . ."

"You know I want to kiss you." Will's face moved closer, but it stopped some inches from hers. "Kiss me, Baby. Put your arms around my neck and kiss me."

Her hands rose to his shoulders. Her eyes became dreamy as doubts faded. "Did you bring me way out here to have your way with me, Will Lang?"

His mouth brushed hers. "No, but it's a thought." A grin flashed briefly. "Just kidding. I'm not that kind of man."

"I'm not that kind of woman, Will."

They'd spoken in different tones, Will's voice containing fun, Clover's sounding deadly serious. He raised his head and looked at her. "I know you're not. You're special, Clover. I knew that the minute I set eyes on you."

"Did you?"

They studied each other. "What did you know when you saw me?" he asked softly. "What did you think?"

"I . . . wondered who you were." What she'd done was rate him a perfect ten, but she couldn't tell him that.

"I had an advantage," Will admitted. "I knew who you were right away." He brought his hands up to her face and placed one on each of Clover's cheeks. "Billy told me you were pretty, but I never imagined your looking like you do. I never imagined you as so special, Baby."

"That awful nickname," she whispered.

"I like it. I like you."

"Yes," she said huskily. "I like you, too."

His mouth came down to hers, gently caressing. Inhaling sharply, Will lifted his head to see into her eyes. "You stir me, Clover. You touch something in me that I wasn't sure was even there."

"I can probably... say the same."

"Are we falling in love?" Will whispered.

"Don't say that! It's too soon."

"All right, I won't rush things. But something's happening with us, honey." Will kissed the right corner of her mouth, and then, with his breath catching, fit his lips to hers for a real kiss.

Her mouth shaped to his, opened for him. With her heart beating wildly, she accepted his tongue and his deep, drugging kiss. His mouth played with hers, his tongue probed for hers. His hands left her face and went around her, drawing her closer to him, ultimately urging her from the rock to the ground.

The kissing went on and on, one melting into another. Somehow they were lying on the grass, with Clover on her back and Will over her. Her fingers explored the crisp hairs just above his shirt collar. Inside she felt like drooping cotton candy, all sugary and syrupy and losing form and texture.

There was wonder in Clover's response. Will's fingers in her hair were as affecting as his kiss on her lips. So was the hot weight of his body on hers. His arms were hard, she realized, his arms and thighs and chest, strong and hard. And yet his hard body inflicted no discomfort on hers, but rather, it seemed to mold to her contours.

"Clover..." He was looking at her with a strange, yearning expression, his mouth glistening like morning dew. "Maybe...maybe we'd better go back to camp."

Her chest felt constricted, as if tightly bound with cording, and she wasn't breathing evenly. "Yes, maybe we'd better." She saw a muscle clench in his jaw. Going back to camp wasn't what he wanted to do at all.

It wasn't what she wanted, either. Not when her body was aching and making outrageous demands. Not when she hated the thought of relaxing her arms and letting him go.

He didn't move and kept looking at her. "I want to make love to you."

She sucked in a quick breath. "I know." How could she not know, when the proof of his desire was burning her belly through two layers of denim, and the essence of his kisses still laid on her lips?

Will gave a funny little laugh. "I don't know how to behave with you. I want you and I feel you want me, too. Yet I'm afraid to proceed." Abruptly he moved away from her and got to his feet. He offered a hand. "Come on, let's go back." Somehow he managed a grin. "It's time to show you what I can do with fresh trout."

Clover let herself be led along. What had he meant about not knowing how to behave with her? He was afraid to proceed? Should she interpret his remarks to mean that he went much faster with other women? If she were someone other than Billy Dove's daughter, would they still be on the grass by that big rock, naked and making love?

Will wasn't very talkative on the walk back, merely pointing out obstructions on the ground that might cause

Clover a problem, should she miss seeing them. She hoped the rapport they'd been enjoying before their petting session hadn't been damaged, for she valued that as highly as she did Will's kisses. Oh, his kisses, she thought weakly. Every other kiss she'd ever received had been a pale, even pitiful imitation when compared to Will's. She must stop thinking about his kisses!

But she learned in practically the next heartbeat that she wasn't the only one remembering. Near an enormous cedar tree on the bank of the creek, Will pulled her against himself. His eyes contained a smoldering light.

"Maybe I do know how to proceed," he whispered raggedly, and kissed her fiercely.

She gasped at the explosion of emotion in her system, standing on tiptoe to kiss him back with a feverish passion. Their arms wound tightly around each other, as though they couldn't get close enough. Her breasts were flattened by the pressure of his chest, and he tucked her hips forward, mating their lower bodies in a way that left no room for innocent conjecture.

He looked purely miserable when he stopped kissing her to suck in air. "God, Clover, you're making me crazy!" He let go of her so suddenly, she nearly fell over.

"*I'm* making *you* crazy?" she gasped and reached out to the massive cedar for support. With one hand on the cedar's trunk, she tried to look as stunned as she felt. She was making him crazy? What in thunderation did he think he was doing to her? She wasn't sure if she knew up from down at that moment. She could hardly breathe and her stomach ached, and sensible or not, if he kissed her again, she'd rip the clothes from his body!

He raked his hair. "Come on. We can't stay out here."

"And camp is going to be safer?"

"What?" Will looked at her oddly, then deliberately tore his gaze away and looked at the sky. She was beautiful, but there was more than Clover Dove's beauty driving him bonkers. He'd always figured that he had only a normal sex drive, but Clover was making him think that his system had somehow become overloaded with hormones. Wanting a woman was one thing; wanting to tear off her clothes in the woods in broad daylight was brand-new to him.

But she was right. Camp wasn't going to alleviate the throbbing in his groin. Only one thing would do that.

"Look," he said, striving for some sort of logic. "This camping trip isn't going to work if we keep fooling around. No more, okay?"

Clover nearly laughed, albeit nervously. Who had started kissing whom? She saw that Will was trying to keep a lid on his feelings, and she managed to maintain a reasonably impassive expression.

"By all means," she murmured huskily.

"And don't talk in that sexy voice!"

"I beg your pardon!"

He held up his hands. "Sorry, forget I said that. I'm not myself. Let's keep walking, okay?"

Clover followed, but she couldn't prevent a smile behind Will's back. As worked up as she herself was, it was still possible to enjoy Will's discomfort—knowing, with some purely feminine glee, that a man like him wanted her so badly.

No one ever had, she realized. But then, she'd never participated so eagerly as she'd just done with Will. If the truth be told, she'd never really wanted a man before.

And she wanted Will Lang. She wanted to undress him, and to have him undress her. It raised her temperature by noticeable degrees to plod along behind Will, envisioning his marvelous behind and long legs without clothes.

Envisioning the *front* of him without clothes made her mind reel, and she caught herself just in time to keep from tripping over a branch on the path.

They were almost back to the campsite when Will stopped walking. "Listen."

"To what?"

"Voices. There are people at our camp." He began jogging. "Come on. No telling who came along."

Clover sighed and continued at the same speed. But a few minutes later she nearly swallowed her teeth when she walked into the clearing and saw her parents. "Billy! Francine!"

Will was smiling weakly. "Nice surprise, Clover."

Francine gave her daughter an energetic hug. "We couldn't figure out where you two went."

"For a hike, Mother."

"That's what Will just explained. When Billy said he had to see Will, I thought we might as well come out here. It's been ages since I've been to Bear Creek. Oh, it's pretty. Isn't it pretty, honey?"

Francine's question was directed to her husband, who enclosed her in one arm for a squeeze. "Sure is, Frannie."

Well, at least they were friends, Clover thought with a sigh and a glance at Will, who looked completely helpless. It was pretty clear to her that Will wasn't overly thrilled about the older Doves' arrival, which made her feel cheated, since she was going to miss what could quite possibly have been the most exciting night of her life.

"How long are you staying?" Clover inquired of her mother.

Francine's smile stretched from ear to ear. "All night, Baby. Isn't that great? We can sit around the camp fire tonight and tell ghost stories."

"Yes, great," Clover agreed faintly.

"You've got enough food and things, don't you, Will?" Billy asked.

"Got plenty of everything, Billy," Will replied. "A little short on sleeping space, but I guess you and I can share a tent and the women can take the other."

"Sure thing," Billy readily agreed.

Francine, wearing a burnt orange pantsuit and pounds of gold jewelry beamed all over the place. "Oh, this is such fun! Clover, honey, where can I put my suitcase?"

"In the largest tent, Mother."

Will was busily digging out pans and utensils, Clover saw with a sigh. Apparently he was going to cook the trout.

Billy made up beds and got Francine settled in with a whole lot of smacking kisses. When they were friends, they were as lovey-dovey as a newly married couple. But when they weren't, everyone better watch out, Clover thought wryly.

Deep down she was greatly relieved that her parents were bosom buddies again. But she couldn't help the thread of resentment that kept her inches away from a truly hearty welcome.

"Can I help?" she asked Will.

"Sure. Mix up about half a cup of cornmeal with a cup of flour and toss in some salt and pepper. Shake it up in one of those plastic bags and then dump it into that flat pan."

Francine's remark about Billy needing to see Will came to Clover while she followed Will's recipe. Billy had just seen Will only last night, so what had brought him out here this evening?

None of the five cleaned trout were huge, but there would be enough, Clover decided. Will opened a large can of black-eyed peas and put them on the propane stove to heat, adding bits of bacon and onion to the pot. He set Clover to work grating cabbage for coleslaw. The camp-out meal was going to be good.

Billy walked over to his car and came out with an acoustical guitar. "Did you bring your guitar, Will?" he called.

Will shook his head. "Nope."

"Well, I just happened to bring two," Billy said, hauling a second instrument from the back seat. He carried both guitars over to Will. "Here, take one and let's pick a little."

"I'm cooking, Billy."

"Heck, the cooking will keep. Come on, Will, let's show the ladies what we can do."

Clover smiled curiously. "Please play, Will. I'd like to hear you."

"Well . . . all right." Will wiped his hands on his pants legs and accepted one of Billy's guitars. He fiddled around some, tuning the strings, then picked a fast run of notes that widened Clover's eyes.

"Looks like you know your way around a guitar," she remarked.

"Heck, he's as good as Pudge was. Almost," Billy added with a teasing twinkle in his eyes.

They decided on a song and Will played a lead-in for Billy to pick up with chords and voice. While Billy sang and strummed, Will filled in the background. His fingers hardly appeared to move over the strings, and yet his music was incredible.

Clover sat down to enjoy the impromptu concert. Will was as good as any guitar picker she'd ever heard. Francine was grinning and tapping her toe, and when the two men struck the last note, she clapped her hands exuberantly. "Hell's bells, you're good, Will Lang! Billy told me you were, but guess I had to hear it for myself."

Will held out the guitar. "Your turn, Francine."

"I've got an idea," Billy declared, and put his guitar in Francine's hands. "Do that new song you wrote, Frannie. Let's see what Will does with the background."

Beaming, Francine positioned the guitar against herself and said, "It's a ballad, Will. Play me some pretty backup, okay?"

Clover saw Will's quiet sigh, and smiled softly at his reluctant resignation. Francine began playing and singing. Will listened for a moment, then began to fill in. It was beautiful. Francine was famous for her sentimental lyrics and pretty melodies, and Clover had no doubt that this new song of her mother's would be an enormous hit.

But it was Will that Clover was watching. He played so effortlessly, as though his fingers functioned as separate entities from the rest of his body. He had wonderful hands, creative hands, Clover thought. She must make a point of seeing some of his cabinetry, which was probably as elegant as his music.

When the song was over, Francine shook her head, as though thoroughly amazed. "That was delightful, Will."

"Told you so," Billy said triumphantly, drawing a peculiar look from Clover. There was something slightly odd about her parents' impulsive trip out here. What did Billy have to see Will about that couldn't keep for another day?

Will put down the guitar. "I'm going to cook those trout. Billy, you and Francine do the entertaining, okay?"

Clover got up to help. Her interest in Will Lang kept expanding. Just looking at him warmed and stirred her emotions. His every smile and grin and facial expression brought him a little closer to her soul. She felt as if they were communicating without saying anything even remotely personal. *I want you, Clover Dove. I want what you want, Will Lang.*

Aloud, Will complimented her on the fine way she wielded the grater, even though she did grate the entire head of cabbage and ended up with enough slaw to feed an army. A little aside from the cooking area, Billy and Francine strummed and sang—and argued.

Clover caught the gist of the debate. "That song should be played in four-four time, Frannie," her father asserted.

"It most certainly should not! It's a waltz, Billy!"

"Yeah, I know, but try it in four-four."

"I'm not trying a waltz in four-four!"

They never had been able to get along if each of them was holding a guitar. Clover sighed, but made no comment, and if Will noticed the relatively mild altercation going on between Billy and Francine, he didn't let on.

Between Will and Clover, they got dinner cooked and the table set. "Come and get it," Will called as he transferred sizzling trout from the frying pan to the plates.

The food was great, especially the trout. Will had coated the fish with the flour and cornmeal mixture, added just a little lemon juice while it was browning, then threw in a generous handful of slivered almonds.

"We could do a little fishing yet tonight," Billy said around a bite of the delicious trout.

"No fishing," Francine said positively. "I want a camp fire."

"I brought a bag of marshmallows," Clover put in.

"Roasted marshmallows!" Francine exclaimed. "Wonderful. That's what we'll do, Billy, sit around the camp fire and roast marshmallows."

Clover looked at Will and received such a beautiful smile from him, her appetite threatened to disappear. If her parents hadn't come along, she and Will would be eating alone. Then, later, with a fire, they would…they might…

It was pretty clear in her mind what they would do, and from the simmering light in Will's marvelous eyes, his thoughts were going in the same direction.

The idea was magical, mysterious, incredible. She actually wanted to make love with a man. Complete love. The next time her girlfriends discussed men, she would know what they were talking about.

To know what her friends did wasn't Clover's motivation, though, not even close. What was prompting such unusual thoughts was Will, himself. His aura, his personality.

His kisses.

But how would he feel about being the first man to have her? Would he think she was some kind of misfit? That maybe no other man had been attracted enough to try something with her?

Or would Will be pleased?

The sun was going down before the dishes were done. Will got busy and built a big fire in the old fire pit. Billy and Francine got out the guitars again, and took up the same argument as before.

Clover helped Will cut some long sticks for the marshmallows, and in the near-darkness, behind a bush, he put his arms around Clover. Eagerly she kissed him back. His mouth on hers made her see stars. His body against hers created a longing that weakened her knees.

"Will you stay a few days at the house when we get back?" Will whispered.

"I . . . don't know."

"You can't run off. We need some time together." His hands drifted down her back to her hips. "I know things are happening fast with us, but don't be afraid."

"I'm not . . . afraid." Clover laughed weakly. "Maybe I am. You're right about this being fast."

"Clover? Will?" a voice echoed through the trees. "Let's have those marshmallows, kids!"

"That's Francine." Clover sighed.

Will hugged her closer and sought her lips again. When they broke apart after a long, thrilling kiss, neither was very steady. "We'd better get those sticks," he muttered.

The roasted marshmallows were delicious, and everyone ate until the bag was empty. Billy passed out the guitars again, insisting that Will play one, and everyone sang. It ended up a pleasant evening, with lots of laughs and good-natured kidding.

Will was the first one to mention bedtime. Clover was yawning by then and glad to retire. Will went to the smaller tent and Clover went to the larger, noticing as she left that Billy and Francine were laying more wood on the fire. They might stay up for hours yet, Clover knew, as neither of her parents ever went to bed early.

Clover undressed by lantern light and put on her pajamas. She was just about to crawl into her sleeping bag when Will ducked into the tent. She gaped, because she never could have imagined Will just popping in like that. "Hi," he said softly. "I'll never get to sleep without a proper good-night."

"And what," she whispered, "do you consider to be a proper good-night?"

"I'll show you." Will turned down the lantern until the flame died. Clover's heart went wild. He groped his way in the dark to sit beside her on the sleeping bag.

"Will . . . Francine and Billy—"

"Are right outside. Don't worry. Proper good-nights don't include anything improper. Not completely improper, anyway." Will reached for her, held her close and breathed in the arousing scent of her hair. "Oh, damn, Clover, you do things to me that no man deserves."

"You don't like what I do to you?"

"I like it," Will groaned. "That's the problem. I like it too much." His hands smoothed over her back. "Lie down."

"Lie down?" she echoed in a shaky voice.

"I can't show you a proper good-night sitting up."

"On top of the sleeping bag?"

"The top's fine, unless you're cold."

"Believe me," Clover whispered, "I'm not cold."

Will chuckled. "Neither am I, Baby, neither am I."

They stretched out, with Clover's head on Will's left arm. Billy's and Francine's voices were audible from outside. It felt naughty to be lying with a man in the dark with people not too far from the tent, especially Clover's parents. But the thrill of lying in Will Lang's arms wasn't to be denied. Her heart was pounding, as was his. She felt him unbuttoning his shirt, and then he took her hand and put it on his bare chest.

"Oh, Will," she whispered, and splayed her fingers into the patch of hair she felt. She gasped softly when his hand slid beneath her pajama top.

"Your skin feels like hot satin," he said low and hoarsely. His mouth moved over her face until he found her lips, and in seconds they were both breathing hard and groping for further intimacy.

He touched one breast, then the other, teasing her nipples with feathery strokes. "Oh, Baby, you're so beautiful," he whispered. His hand opened and held one breast, kneading it gently. She moaned deep in her chest and pressed her lips to the rapidly beating pulse at the base of his throat.

She felt his hand skim down her belly and go into the elastic waistband of her pajama bottoms. "Will...we can't..."

"We're not, don't worry. I only want to touch you."

What he wanted to "touch" was suddenly aching unmercifully. She spread her thighs willingly and let him explore what no man ever had. Heat rose in her body, heat and need and the most incredible sensation of belonging to this man. He was trembling, but so was she.

He laid back suddenly, breathing hard, and tried to make a small joke. "Guess there's no such thing as 'proper' with you, Miss Clover."

"Miss Clover" wasn't very happy. Her hands clenched into fists and she felt an almost unbearable urge to scream. She swallowed and tried to calm her racing blood. She knew without question that she was feeling exactly what Will did—intense physical desire and frustration. It was a remarkable sensation, albeit an uncomfortable one.

She *would* stay with Will after they left Bear Creek tomorrow and returned to his house, Clover decided. Their's was not a trivial passion, and she was not going to return to Nashville and take up her life as though nothing had happened out here.

"Go, Will," she whispered unevenly. "Go to your own tent."

He sat up, wanting to kiss and touch her again but knowing that if he did nothing would stop him, not even Billy and Francine outside arguing by the fire.

"Good night, Baby. Try to sleep well."

"You, too. Try."

He laughed with some cynicism and left through the flap.

Six

The next morning Clover slept through her mother getting up, which was unusual as she was normally a fairly light sleeper. But the tent was empty when she awakened; Francine was elsewhere.

Lying there within the soft folds of her sleeping bag, a smile touched Clover's lips. She'd dreamed of Will during the night. Or, more accurately, an exciting, dark-haired man had slipped in and out of a few memorable scenes and he must have been Will. Who else would be invading her dreams at the present time? Certainly not that guy with the gold boots and purple-and-white zebra-striped pants back in Nashville!

Will Lang. Handsome, sweet, sexy man. A breathy sigh lifted Clover's bosom. Never had she been hit so hard, so fast. There was significance and importance connected to Will, and the whole thing struck Clover as strange but nice. A few days ago Will was no more than a memory, and not an especially appealing one, at that. Now the mere thought of him made her feel extremely female and . . . what? Was it happiness coursing through her veins? Yes, she decided after a brief internally directed examination. She honestly felt as though she couldn't smile enough.

The camp was quiet. Clover listened for a moment then got up and peeked through the flap. Francine was sitting near the fire with a cup of coffee. Will and Billy were nowhere in sight.

"Morning," Francine called brightly as she spotted her daughter.

"Good morning. Where are Billy and Will?"

"Fishing. You slept in."

Clover stepped from the tent and indulged in a leisurely, languorous stretch. "Sleeping outdoors is marvelous."

Francine put a bit of wryness in a grin. "Well, I'm not sure I agree with that observation."

"Didn't you sleep well?" Clover picked up a mug from the table and poured herself some coffee. Sipping, she registered her mother's perfect hair and full makeup. Today's outfit was bright green pants and blouse, and the gold jewelry was well in place.

"I hardly slept a wink," Francine confided. "I'm not much for roughing it anymore, Baby."

"Did you have breakfast?"

"Will made pancakes and your father ate, of course. I had my usual, some fresh fruit. There's pancake batter left and the griddle's right there, if you want some."

"Later," Clover said. "I think I'll clean up first."

"There's no hurry. Billy said not to expect them for a few hours."

"In that case I'll finish my coffee." Clover sank into one of the chairs and propped her bare feet up on a rock. "I was really surprised to see you and Billy yesterday."

"Yes, well, we're surprising people."

Clover laughed. "No argument there, Mother."

"You like Will, don't you?"

"Yes, I like him." Behind the admission was a realization that she didn't mind admitting affection for Will Lang. She rather enjoyed admitting it, as a matter of fact. "What do you think of Will, Mother?"

Francine stirred in her chair. "Well . . . he's a handsome devil."

"Yes, but do you like him?" Clover waved her hand. "There are a lot of handsome men, Francine, if that's all a woman is looking for."

"You've only known him a few days."

"Does that matter? How long did you and Billy know each other before you got married? Seems like I remember you saying something about three weeks."

Francine cleared her throat. "Are you thinking about marriage?"

Clover laughed. "Heavens, no! As you pointed out, it's only been a few days. But I doubt that time means very much if two people really fall in love." Her laughter faded. "I don't believe that I'm in love with Will, but I do like him." Clover stopped to wonder about that last comment. There was more than "liking" in her system, even if labeling the feeling as "love" was premature.

She saw in the next breath that Francine didn't appear to be very comfortable. "What's wrong? Is there something about Will Lang that I should know?"

Francine fidgeted for a moment. "Baby, I had no idea . . . when we came up here, I mean."

"You didn't intrude, if that's what you're hinting at, Mother."

"No, no, it's nothing like that. But..." Setting her cup down on the ground beside her chair, Francine got up. "Clover, sweetie, I'm afraid you're not going to like...oh, drat!"

Clover sat up straighter. Something was prickling Francine, and it had to do with Will. Was there some sort of awful secret in his past, something that Billy and Francine knew but she did not? Clover searched her memory for a clue, a conversation, perhaps, a remark that might have gone in one ear and out the other before seeing Will again.

"Please tell me what's bothering you," she said quietly, afraid to hear what was on Francine's mind but more afraid of not hearing it.

Francine sighed. "I guess there's a chance that it might not affect you too much."

"Mother, what is it?" There was a touch of impatience in Clover's voice. The topic was making her nervous.

"Honey..." Francine stopped, then blurted, "Billy wants Will to join his band. You see," she rushed on, "Gus Breen received an offer to record an album of his own songs. He feels badly about leaving Billy in the lurch, but he's going to be terribly involved and...well, you can see the problem."

Gus Breen had been Billy's lead guitar man since Pudge's death. Oddly Francine's information didn't cause Clover any alarm. In fact, it was quite relieving. She'd feared hearing any number of things, most of which revolved around women.

"He won't take the job," Clover declared.

"You don't think so?"

"He's not an entertainer, Mother. A musician, yes, but not an entertainer."

"Well, I suppose. But Billy can be very persuasive."

Francine was right. Billy could be persuasive, and not only that, he was important to Will. Clover felt a sprouting discomfort. If Will got into the music business, he would be just like everyone else she knew. Resentment arose. Darn it! Billy knew she was interested in Will.

No, Billy did *not* know that—not for a fact, he didn't. They'd discussed Will, with Billy touting his younger friend's steady ways. But Billy couldn't possibly know how quickly Clover's attitude toward Will was changing and warming.

"Clover, honey, does Will know how you feel about him?"

"There isn't anything to know," Clover said quickly. "We're friends, nothing more."

"Baby, you mentioned marriage," Francine reminded gently.

"Only in regard to you and Billy. Really, Mother, I never meant to give you the wrong impression. If Will decides to join Billy's band, it's nothing to me."

"Are you sure?"

"Very sure. Now, I think I'll go wash up in the creek. Which way did Billy and Will go? I'll go in the opposite direction."

"They went upstream," Francine replied. "But there's warm water in that big pot if you want to bathe in the tent."

"The creek will be fine, thanks."

Clover delayed thinking about Will until she'd gathered up clean clothes, soap, a towel and her toothbrush. As she made her way through the brush to the creek, though, she couldn't ignore Francine's information any longer.

What if Will accepted Billy's offer? For whatever reason, be it friendship or Billy's powers of persuasion? Then

Will wouldn't be living in that old house, nor making jokes about a pay phone in his backyard. He'd have to give up his woodworking. He'd travel a lot and probably stay in Nashville when he wasn't on the road.

He would not be the same man.

But how could she protest?

She couldn't. Will owed her nothing. She was in no position to even mention her preferences, let alone hope that he would abide by them. She would say nothing should Will announce plans to join Billy's band.

But neither would she get further involved with Will. If he wished to be an entertainer, that was his prerogative. It was hers to avoid a romantic entanglement with a musician.

Clover's determination faltered. She dated men from the entertainment world at times, but she couldn't see herself dating Will if he joined their ranks. Why not?

The answer was simple, of course. She liked Will. Maybe she already loved him a little.

"Oh, damn," she whispered, and immediately attempted to bolster her flagging spirits by telling herself not to jump to conclusions. Will might turn Billy down. He might say, "Billy, I'm pleased you thought of me, and I thank you for the offer, but I'm content with my life as it is."

While bathing in the cold creek water, Clover urged patience upon herself. *Give Will every benefit of the doubt. Don't second-guess him. Wait and see what he does. Don't, for God's sake, think the worst!*

When the fishermen returned with only two small trout, Clover's heart sank—the meager catch seemed to be proof that Billy and Will had done more talking than fishing.

They were in good spirits, particularly Billy, which also felt as if it were some kind of proof to Clover.

She greeted both men, as Francine did. No one mentioned music, and while Clover was dying to know the outcome of Will's and Billy's discussion, she kept her intense curiosity to herself.

Everyone pitched in to make lunch, and then all four sat down and enjoyed the sandwiches and fruit and soft drinks. Clover kept eyeing her father, wondering if Billy looked a little more elated than he would if Will had turned him down. It was hard to tell with Billy. He had a natural twinkle in his eyes and a disarming grin, attractive traits that no doubt contributed to his widespread popularity.

Clover studied all three of her companions, who were exchanging jokes and laughing. Her parents were both attractive, extremely talented people. So was Will. Maybe he was a lot more like Billy and Francine than she'd thought. Maybe she was the only person here who didn't think fame was the only goal worth pursuing.

Billy got to his feet. "Time for us to be heading home, honey," he said to Francine.

Will got up to help Billy carry his and Francine's things to the car. Clover began putting food away, noticing that her father and Will had a few quiet words near the trunk of the Mercedes. She knew then, as surely as she knew her own name, that Will had agreed to play guitar in Billy's band. Her stomach turned over, and she was glad that she hadn't eaten a big lunch.

After hugs all around, Billy and Francine drove away. Will immediately came to Clover and attempted to pull her into his arms with a murmured, "Now, where were we last night?"

Smiling sickishly, Clover eluded the embrace. "I think we should go, too, Will."

He looked puzzled. "Anything wrong?"

She could not say it. If her life depended on a reference to Will and music, she would fall over on the spot. "Of course not," she lied with an almost normal smile on her face. "It's just time to go."

Will hesitated for a moment, then nodded. "All right. I'll break down the tents and start loading the truck."

It took nearly an hour, but finally everything was on the truck, including every speck of trash. When Clover and Will drove away, the campsite was exactly as it had been on their arrival, natural and debris free.

Will sent her a smile. "It was fun, wasn't it?"

"Yes."

Clover was looking straight ahead. "Baby, is something bothering you?"

She shaped a perfect smile. "No, of course not."

Will took his right hand from the wheel and patted the seat. "Move over and sit beside me."

"And leave my seat belt behind?" Clover spoke lightly, a strain to accomplish when she felt so tight inside.

"There's one in the middle, too."

"No, I think I should sit here and you should keep your mind on the road."

Will frowned. Last night she would have gladly sat closer to him and today he sensed distance in Clover's attitude. There *was* something wrong, but what?

Confused by her withdrawal, he resorted to teasing. "By the way, you never did beg me to marry you, and I know you loved my trout."

"Your trout were fabulous, but I'm not ready for marriage. Guess you'll just have to stay single for a while longer, Will Lang."

Her teasing wasn't nearly as funny as he supposed his was. For one thing, there was an underlying seriousness in her voice, that same sense of distance he'd been picking up.

Will mentally searched for a topic to bring her out of her mood. Besides, there was something he wanted her to know. Since Billy had brought up the subject of being in his band, Will had been thinking that it would please Clover, although, to be perfectly honest, he wasn't sure it pleased him. Whatever, he hadn't told Billy no. "I've got some news," he said.

"Oh?" Clover's cheerful expression was a complete lie. She knew exactly what Will's "news" was, and she'd been wondering if and when he would mention it.

"Billy asked me to join his band for a while. Gus Breen's got other plans and is leaving the group."

Clover waited for further information and finally said, "And?"

"Well . . . it wasn't an easy decision, but I told Billy I'd help him out."

"How nice for Billy," Clover murmured. "And for you, too, of course."

Will concentrated on her reaction. "I'll be in Nashville a lot. We can see each other often."

Clover cleared her throat. "I suppose."

Will laughed, a trifle uneasily. She was pleased, wasn't she? "Don't sound so eager."

"Will, I've been doing a lot of thinking. You and I were moving much too fast. I'm not ready for . . . well, you know."

Were moving much too fast? Will felt his stomach turn over. "For commitment?"

"I guess that word's as good as any."

"And you did all of that thinking during the night?"

"Most of it, yes."

Will took his eyes from the road to look at her. "Are you telling me that you don't want to see me again?"

Clover squirmed on the seat. "We'll see each other, Will, how could we not? If you're working with Billy and in Nashville a lot, we're bound to run into each other."

"That *is* what you're telling me!" Will spoke with amazement, because after yesterday he couldn't have imagined this happening. He managed a shaky laugh. "I thought we were getting along great."

"We were. We *are!*" The depth of emotion in Will's voice shook Clover. Regardless of her own negative feelings on the matter of Will getting involved in the music business, she had no desire to see him unhappy. She couldn't explain, though. Explaining would be similar to telling him how to live his life, and that was something she would never do. He'd made his decision and she would accept it. He, by the same token, would have to accept hers.

"Friendship is always valuable, Will."

"So we're only friends now." Will smirked. "I'd sure like to know what the hell went through your mind last night to change it so completely. Yesterday you weren't thinking of me as a friend, Clover."

Clover's chin came up. "Yesterday I behaved impulsively. So did you."

"But I don't regret it, and you do."

He was getting angry, which made Clover uneasy. "Maybe we should change the subject."

"Change the subject, hell! I want to know why I was damned near a lover yesterday and today I'm a friend!"

"I came to my senses!" Clover said sharply. "I don't fall in bed with any man who hints at doing so, Will Lang!"

"I never thought you did!"

"But you're mad about it!"

"Yes, I'm mad, but not because you didn't fall in bed with me." Will calmed his voice. "Clover, you owe me a better explanation than having come to your senses. Hell, there wasn't anything *not* sensible about what nearly happened yesterday. If Billy and Francine hadn't come along, we would have made love last night."

Clover turned her suddenly flaming face to the side window. "I'm not so sure about that."

Will drew a long, exasperated breath. "You're damned puzzling, do you know that?"

Clover fell silent, but her emotions were too torn up for her to remain so for long. "I'm not trying to confuse you or anyone else. The concept is very simple. I'm not ready for a love affair, which is what you were thinking about yesterday and last night in the tent."

"Don't judge my motives, Clover. You're not a mind reader and you don't know what I was thinking. For your information, I never once put you and the word 'affair' in the same thought."

"All right, fine. Let's leave it at that."

"And that's the end of it, right?" Will said with some bitterness.

"I don't see why you're so angry. A few days ago we didn't even know each other."

"That's right, we didn't. But don't try to convince me that something wasn't happening with us. Maybe I'll never know what changed your mind, but I don't believe for a minute that you had some damned revelation in the night."

Clover faced him. For a moment she had to fight the strongest urge to tell him the truth. Honesty was right on the tip of her tongue, but she bit it back and said instead, "That's all that happened, whether you want to believe it or not."

Neither of them said another word until they pulled into Will's yard. He parked the pickup and turned off the engine. "Clover—?"

"I'll be leaving right away," she said quickly, forestalling another attempt by Will to pick her mind.

His face shut down. "That's just about what I figured." Getting out of the truck and slamming the door, Will moved things around in the pickup bed and hauled out her suitcase, which he carried over to her car. "Do you have anything in the house?"

"No, everything's in the suitcase."

And suddenly, just like that, she hated what was happening. Yesterday she'd been as close to falling in love as she'd ever come; today she felt miserably unhappy. "Will, I'm sorry."

Will studied her with a tense expression. "I'm sorry, too. I don't know what for, but I apologize for whatever it was I did to change things so drastically."

Sighing, Clover looked away. "Well...I'd better get going. It's a long drive."

Will stowed her suitcase in the trunk after Clover unlocked and opened it, then followed as she got behind the wheel. He held the door open and bent over to see in. "I'll call you when I get to Nashville."

Clover sent him a glance and then concentrated on putting the key into the ignition. "Call if you want."

He hesitated then stood back and closed the door. The engine turned over and caught. Clover knew that she'd hurt Will. He didn't understand her attitude reversal in the slightest.

But she couldn't explain. For that matter, other than knowing that she couldn't get involved with a music man, she had no explanation. And Will had every right to play music or to do anything else that caught his fancy.

With a farewell wave, she turned the car around and drove out of Will's yard. She felt like bawling, but that was no one's business but her own.

Seven

_____

"*Miss Clover? This is your friend and admirer, Will Lang. I'm in Nashville now, staying with Billy for a few days, just until I can find my own place. I'd be honored if you'd give me a call when you have the time. Sure would like to say hello in person.*"

At the first sound of Will's voice—deep and steady, even with that familiar teasing note—on her answering machine, Clover's ears pricked up. She had pressed the Play button rather absently and listened through several other messages while thumbing through the day's mail.

Clover set the mail on the counter with a sinking sensation. Will was finally in Nashville and staying with her parents. She thought she'd handled the distance between them reasonably well. For a week and a half she'd attended luncheons with friends, had a few dinners out, also with friends, worked her usual hours for the usual charities and put in several long days at the recording studio.

Throughout the almost constant activity, she'd kept Will
Lang pretty much at bay. It was not going to be quite so
easy to do from here on in.

Most worrisome was the fact that Clover had no defi-
nite game plan in mind where Will was concerned. It hurt
to think about him and she avoided doing so. Although,
she had found herself wondering why she'd been destined
to finally be genuinely attracted to a man, supposing him
completely unattached from the music world, and then
have him suddenly plunge into that very career. It was
ironic and irritating and saddening, all at the same time.

It was also painfully apparent that she'd come dangerously close to falling in love with Will Lang. Playing lead
guitar in Billy Dove's band would result in anything but
anonymity for Will. As talented and good-looking as he
was, the fans would make him a star, never mind Will's
own personal goals. That was not the future she hoped to
secure for herself.

Clover glanced at the clock on the stove, which indicated a few minutes after 6:00 p.m. Billy might be home,
although Francine had left Nashville with her band members for a three-week tour.

Sometimes answering machines were a pain in the neck.
Without one there was a chance that Will's calls would
never catch her at home, which would take decision-
making out of her hands. A recorded message put her on
the spot. Ignoring it would be rude, and she disliked the
idea of rudeness with Will.

Clover was trying hard not to resent her father's role in
Will's transformation. Without Billy's offer—and, undoubtedly, his impassioned plea—Will would still be
building cabinets and living in the woods. But she really
couldn't blame Billy too much, not after hearing Will play.
It was only natural that Billy had thought of Pudge's son

to replace Gus Breen in the band. It was a wonder, actually, that Billy hadn't coaxed Will into joining his group of excellent musicians before this.

Clover reached for the phone, then drew back. She should return Will's call, but what if he asked her out?

The telephone rang, startling her, and she let it ring until the answering machine picked up the call. A bright female voice said, "This is Annie, Clover. Call me when—"

Clover grabbed the phone. Annie Cooper was a longtime friend. "I'm here, Annie. Just came in."

"Clover! Glad I caught you, sweetie. Listen, I'm in a hurry, but I had to ask you something. I ran into Billy today and there was the greatest looking guy with him I've ever seen. His name's Will Lang, and Billy said you knew him. What's the lowdown, friend of mine? Who is he?"

Clover sat down hard, with her stomach feeling as though it was dropping lower than even the chair's level. Annie Cooper was a doll, an *aggressive* doll, and the thought of her sinking her well-manicured claws into Will Lang was a blow Clover hadn't seen coming.

She tried to sound casual. "Will's an old family friend, Annie. Maybe you remember his father, Pudge Lang? Pudge was Billy's lead guitar man for many years."

"Oh, yes, I do remember the name now. So, where's Will been hiding for so long? Honestly, Clover, he's an absolute dream. Umm...you're not interested in him, are you?"

"Interested?"

"Yeah, you know, like man-woman interested? I don't mind telling you that I am, but you did know him first and I'm not one to step on a friend's toes."

Reacting impulsively, Clover squared her shoulders. "As a matter of fact, Annie, I am interested."

"Oh, darn! Well listen, sweetie, I've got to run. If you ever *lose* interest, let me know, okay?"

"Yes, Annie, I'll let you know."

Clover broke the connection and sat there feeling slightly numb. Will was already making a splash. Annie Cooper was only the first woman to notice; she wouldn't be the last.

Gathering her courage, Clover dialed her parents' number. The Dove phone rang until a recorded message came on the line. Clover waited for the beep then said, "This is Clover. I'm returning Will's call."

Three evenings later Clover came home late. She was tired, her slacks and blouse were wrinkled, her hair needed brushing and her makeup was gone. Her part in the recording sessions was over. Everyone had stayed until after eight to finish up. With a meal of Chinese takeout and plans to eat, bathe and hit the sack, Clover pulled into her garage and cut the engine. She gathered her purse and the food and got out of the car. She was about to push the button on the garage wall to lower the door when a man appeared.

"*Eek!*" she cried, and dropped her package of food. "Good Lord, Will! You scared me half to death!"

"Didn't mean to." Will went into the garage and picked up the bulky sack. "What's this?"

"Chinese food. Were you waiting for me?" It was a dumb question, because why else would he be lurking around her garage?

"Chinese, huh? Got enough for two? I missed supper."

With her nerves settling down, Clover recognized gladness in her soul. Wearing a blue Western-cut shirt and snug jeans, Will looked wonderful—tall and handsome and crisply clean. She must make up her mind about Will. Annie Cooper would set her sights on him in a heartbeat.

"Yes, there's plenty for two," she said calmly, belying the thumping excitement of her pulse. The garage door closed with a metallic groan and a bump. "Come in," she said invitingly.

Will followed her through the door connecting her condo's living quarters and garage. "Nice place."

"I like it." Clover proceeded to the kitchen. "Just set that sack on the table. I'm going to take a minute to freshen up, then I'll heat everything in the microwave and we'll eat. Make yourself at home. I won't be long."

"Don't hurry," Will called as she left the kitchen. He looked at the oak cabinets, white appliances and blue tile. The room was bright and pretty and spotlessly clean. Wandering into the neat-as-a-pin living room, he admired the oak tables and blue-upholstered furniture. Spotting another doorway, he peeked in and grinned. This room was obviously a catchall. The TV was in here, as were loaded bookshelves, an easel with a half-finished oil painting of blotchy-looking, colorful flowers, a large canvas bag with what appeared to be knitting supplies, two comfortable recliner chairs and stacks of magazines.

One wall was crowded with photos and snapshots. Will moved closer to take a look at the array. Many were of Billy and Francine. Will recognized some other faces, people who were prominent in the music business. Clover was in several of the shots, and his eyes narrowed as he studied them with circumspection.

She was a pretty woman. A beautiful woman. But as he'd thought before, Clover's looks weren't her only draw. She was different, he decided. Different from any other woman he'd ever known. Extremely spirited and keen-witted. And dangerously sexy.

He'd thought about sex a lot lately, and not just in general terms. His libido was focused on Clover Dove; she was the lady he wanted.

He'd also thought a lot about her abrupt reversal at Bear Creek. It was as if something had turned off her light bulb, and since it had happened after Billy and Francine had shown up, he could only conclude that one or both of them had caused it. They must have said something to turn her off, although what it could have been eluded Will. He hadn't mentioned it to Billy, as he still couldn't bring himself to discuss Clover with her father.

Will settled into one of the recliners and stretched it out to its full-length with a sigh of comfort. He was getting drowsy when he heard Clover looking for him. "Will?"

"In here."

Clover came in. "Oh, you found my messy room."

"It's a great room." Will adjusted the chair to a sitting position. "I didn't know you painted."

Clover dubiously eyed the canvas on the easel. "I'm not very good but I enjoy trying."

Will stood up. "It looks pretty good to me."

Clover smiled. "Thanks. Ready to eat?"

"Sure."

They went to the kitchen, where Clover pulled the cartons from the sack. Will leaned his hips against the counter and folded his arms across his chest. "How've you been?"

Clover sent him a glance. "All right."

"We keep missing each other by telephone. Thought I'd stop that nonsense and just come by. Hope you don't mind."

"How long did you wait for me? I'm not usually so late."

"I waited a while, but I'm not complaining." He'd waited for more than two hours, but it was true that he

NO RISK, NO OBLIGATION TO BUY...NOW OR EVER!

GUARANTEED

PLAY "ROLL A DOUBLE" AND GET AS MANY AS FIVE GIFTS!

HERE'S HOW TO PLAY:

1. Peel off label from front cover. Place it in space provided at right. With a coin, carefully scratch off the silver dice. This makes you eligible to receive two or more free books, and possibly another gift, depending on what is revealed beneath the scratch-off area.

2. You'll receive brand-new Silhouette Desire® novels. When you return this card, we'll rush you the books and gift you qualify for ABSOLUTELY FREE!

3. Then, if we don't hear from you, every month we'll send you 6 additional novels to read and enjoy months before they are available in stores. You can return them and owe nothing, but if you decide to keep them, you'll pay only $2.49* per book—a saving of 40¢ each off the cover price—plus only 69¢ delivery for the entire shipment.

4. When you subscribe to the Silhouette Reader Service™, you'll also get our newsletter, as well as additional free gifts from time to time.

5. You must be completely satisfied. You may cancel at any time simply by sending us a note or a shipping statement marked "cancel" or by returning any shipment to us at our expense.

This lovely heart-shaped box is richly detailed with cut-glass decorations, perfect for holding a precious memento or keepsake—and it's yours absolutely free when you accept our no-risk offer.

SILHOUETTE "NO RISK" GUARANTEE

- You're not required to buy a single book—ever!
- You must be completely satisfied or you may cancel at any time simply by sending us a note or shipping statement marked "cancel" or by returning any shipment to us at our cost. Either way, you will receive no more books; you'll have no obligation to buy.
- The free books and gift you claimed on this "Roll A Double" offer remain yours to keep no matter what you decide.

If offer card is missing, please write to: Silhouette Reader Service, P.O. Box 609, Fort Erie, Ontario L2A 5X3

Business
Reply Mail

No Postage Stamp
Necessary if Mailed
in Canada

Postage will be paid by

SILHOUETTE READER SERVICE
PO BOX 609
FORT ERIE, ONT.
L2A 9Z9

DETACH AND MAIL CARD TODAY!

wasn't complaining. Clover didn't know he was here, after all, and now that he was with her, the wait was trivial.

Damn, she was pretty. She'd put on a gauzy skirt and loose overblouse of the same flowing fabric, and the outfit's creamy color was almost the same shade as her hair. There were cream-and-rose leather sandals on her feet, and her toenails were painted a hot pink.

Just looking at her warmed him.

After heating the food in the microwave, Clover prepared two plates with generous portions of fried rice, sweet-and-sour pork, and chicken chow mein.

Quickly she laid out flatware and napkins on the table. "What would you like to drink? There's iced tea and soda."

"Iced tea, thanks." Will grinned. "I didn't come to beg supper off of you."

"No problem. As you can see, I bought far too much for one person."

Clover brought the two plates to the table. "It's ready. Come and sit down."

"Thanks."

The Chinese food was good, and they ate without comment for a few moments.

"So," Clover said, "how's the music going?"

Will's spirit perked up. He was sure Clover would be interested in that topic. "So far, all I've done is practice. I've got a lot to learn—a whole slew of new songs and Billy's routines and procedures."

"Does Billy have a tour coming up?"

"In a few weeks."

Clover spoke with studied nonchalance. "Do you think you're going to like playing with the band?"

Will hesitated, because he didn't want to disappoint her with the true nature of his feelings, which weren't all that positive. "I don't know. It's sure different than what I'm used to."

"Yes, it is." Hope sprang to life within Clover. Maybe Will wouldn't like the music business. Maybe the endless rehearsals would get him down. If not that, his very first tour might do it. It took a hardy soul and intractable dedication to survive the tours. One-night stands, being dragged from one stage to another, long bus rides, sleeping sitting up a lot of the time, eating greasy food—the thought turned Clover's stomach.

But her parents not only survived such ghastly routines, they thrived on them. Successful entertainers did not cringe from physical discomfort and inconvenience. Apparently applause and public acclaim outweighed the negative aspects of success.

Not for Clover. And only time would tell with Will.

While they ate and chatted, Clover's thoughts ran the gamut. Will was handsome and exciting. Annie Cooper could not have him. But how could she, Clover, keep him from predatory females and not expose herself to heartache?

It was a dilemma she had never before encountered.

"Have you found an apartment?" she questioned.

Will shook his head. "I don't want an apartment. I'm looking for a house."

"To buy?"

"To rent. Know of anything?"

"Afraid not. I'm surprised you want a house."

"I need space, Clover. I need to be able to get outdoors, if for nothing more than to mow a lawn."

Yes, she could see Will mowing a lawn. Shirtless, probably, with the sun glistening in his hair and his skin slick with perspiration.

She drew in a suddenly unsteady breath. Will was not just a friend to her, not when such a mental image could shake her very foundation. For some reason her gaze focused on the pearl-like buttons of his shirt. Behind them, she knew, were concealed snaps. One yank would open the shirt from his sexy throat to his sexy belt buckle.

A hot flush started in her midsection and radiated outward in every direction, heating her pink-crested toes right along with her face. Hastily Clover got up and went for the pitcher of iced tea. Will held up his glass for a refill and asked innocently, "Anything wrong?"

"No, of course not." Clover topped off his glass then splashed tea into her own. She set the pitcher back in the refrigerator and resumed her seat at the table. That's when she suspected that his question hadn't been nearly as innocent as she'd supposed. He was looking at her closely, and if that was innocence in his eyes, she was Wonder Woman!

"What?" she asked sharply.

"I like being with you."

Dammit, what was she going to do? Clover squirmed on her chair. She felt like the proverbial dog in the manger, wanting Will Lang, afraid of wanting him, afraid that if she did what was only sensible and insisted he stay away from her, someone else—Annie Cooper, more than likely—would go after him quicker than a wink. He was not going to live in Nashville for long without female companionship.

Clover sighed. "I like your being here, too."

Will displayed a satisfied smile. "And that foolishness about not seeing each other is a thing of the past, right?"

The truth came out. "Yes, I suppose it is."

"Great." Will got up and went around the table. "Come here," he said softly, holding out his hand.

Clover's insides started leaping around. She stared at the big hand before her. "Will...I didn't mean that we should...get involved."

"A little involvement never hurt anyone, Baby." Will reached down, took her hand and urged her up. Clover teetered on weak legs. His arms went around her and he looked into her eyes. "I've thought of little else but you since you drove away," he said softly.

So much ran through her mind, a swift sweep of emotions and events, speeding up her heart, drying her mouth. He felt incredible, arousing, but she shouldn't stand still and let this happen.

Somehow she managed a rubbery sidestep and escaped the embrace, leaving Will with a surprised expression. "Will, we can see each other...if you want to after this. But I won't be rushed. You have to understand that. I...won't be rushed."

"A kiss would be rushing?"

"A kiss leads to...other things," she mumbled. Other things, yes. Such as hands beneath her clothing, as he'd done that night in her tent. Such as touches too hot to ignore, caresses too provocative to deny. She had a lot to figure out, such as why she didn't want any other woman getting her clutches on Will Lang, even though she was uncertain about her feelings toward him.

"I can't see you without wanting you," Will said quietly.

Clover wet her lips with the tip of her tongue. "You speak so bluntly."

"Not normally. You do funny things to me, Clover. What do you want me to do, pretend that you're one of the guys? You're not. You never will be."

Clover took a stab at levity. "Well, I can't say that I see you as one of the girls."

"That's a start, Baby." Will raked his hair. "Look, whatever's holding you back, I can live with it. You'll figure it out eventually. You like me, I like you. There's something vital between us, something very physical. But that's not all it is, and I intend to find out where it could lead." Will's gaze remained on her face. "If you agree, of course."

"I guess I'd like to find out where it might lead, too," Clover said slowly.

"That's step number two," Will murmured and moved closer. His hand rose to feather a caress to her hair. "Maybe that's what we have to do, honey, take it one step at a time. I never meant to rush you. I've never rushed a woman in my life."

Will was beginning to think that rushing Clover had been the problem at Bear Creek. He'd been going pretty fast, and maybe all that had occurred was that she'd decided to put on the brakes. He could understand that attitude, he even admired it. Fast women had never appealed to him.

Will had been thinking a lot about himself and the fairer sex recently. He'd come to one startling conclusion: William Bradley Lang was a one-woman man. So far in his lifetime, that one special woman hadn't come along. Not unless she was Clover Dove. That's what he kept running up against, the gut feeling that Clover was the one.

And he *had* rushed her at Bear Creek. Not intentionally, not because of some selfish plan to take her to bed. No, everything that happened between them had been spontaneous.

But maybe spontaneity wasn't his best course with Clover, and he could be as patient as Job if necessary.

"You fed me tonight," he said softly. "Will you let me feed you tomorrow night?"

"Dinner?" Clover said huskily. He was so close, and his fingers in her hair were raising goose bumps on her skin.

Will frowned suddenly. "I just remembered. I can't do it tomorrow night. Billy's got a late rehearsal lined up. How about Friday evening?"

Actually Friday would be much better than tomorrow night. The extra time would give her a chance to sort out her crazy-quilt feelings. How on earth could she keep a man like Will from noticing other women unless she let him know that *she* wanted him? He was a healthy, normal male, and making it very clear that he found her desirable, to boot. His attentions were gratifying and provocative, but a woman could string a man along just so much before he gave up and moved on to greener, more cooperative pastures.

Clover smiled faintly. "Friday will be fine."

"Good." Will stood there looking at her and finally murmured, "I sure do like you, Miss Clover." He wanted to kiss and hold her so badly, he ached. But he put on a grin and let his hand fall from her hair. "Seven on Friday evening?"

"Seven's fine."

"Formal or informal? You name it."

"Informal," Clover responded in a strange, slightly choked voice.

"You're a woman after my own heart."

Speaking of hearts, Clover thought after Will had gone, hers was being gradually overcome by Mr. Lang. Why couldn't she just kick him out of her life and go on as though they hadn't met again? Was it because Annie Cooper was waiting in the wings?

God, was she really so petty as to date Will to keep him away from other women?

Later, after the kitchen had been straightened and Clover was in bed, the truth struck without mercy. She cared too much for Will Lang. Annie Cooper, be damned! It wasn't Annie driving her to Will, it was herself! She wanted to be with Will. She wanted to go out with him, laugh with him, talk and tease and flirt with him.

And she wanted to make love with him.

And maybe she would. Just maybe she would do anything and everything with Will Lang!

And there would go all of her hopes and dreams down a well, too. There would be no Mr. Nice, Normal and Anonymous if she got caught up in a mad love affair with a music man.

A tear trickled from Clover's eye, and she let it slide down her temple to the pillow. Just how, in God's name, was she going to resolve the situation?

Eight

"Clover, honey, I'm having a little get-together at the house tomorrow evening, and I'd like you to come. Got to introduce Will to friends and folks," Billy said jovially. "It's a surprise, though, so don't say anything to Will, okay?"

Clover gripped the phone tighter. "Are you sure he wants to be introduced, Billy?"

"Why in heck wouldn't he?"

"Well, I don't know," Clover said with some acerbity. She didn't like the idea of Will meeting Billy's friends and folks, every one of whom was in the music business. "But Will always lived so privately. I just thought he might like to retain *some* of his previous life-style."

"Are you mad about something?"

Clover rolled her eyes but stopped herself from another sharp retort. "Billy, Will asked me out to dinner tomorrow night."

"He did? Hey, that's great, Baby, perfect. After he picks you up, tell him you need to come by and see me for something. You can bring him in and everyone will be waiting."

"I'm not fond of surprise parties, Billy."

"Doggone it, Clover, you *are* mad about something!"

"I am not! But I happen to think that surprise parties are adolescent!"

"Thunderation! Are you gonna help me get Will to the house tomorrow night or not?"

Clover let go of a lungful of exasperated air. "I'll help! I'll help!"

"Good. Thanks. Now, young lady, suppose you tell me what put a burr under your saddle."

"Billy, there's nothing to tell."

"The heck there ain't. This is your old dad you're trying to con, Baby. What's wrong?"

I wish you hadn't talked Will into joining your band! Sighing, Clover repeated that nothing was wrong. "When will Mother be home?"

"Not for another few weeks. I'll be gone before she gets back. Did Will tell you about our upcoming tour?"

"He mentioned it, yes." Clover heard her father chuckle.

"So you and Will are dating. Glad to hear it, honey. Will's as steady as they come."

He was. "So you said. Billy, I've got to go. I'm due at the children's home. Thanks for the invitation. I'll see you tomorrow night."

"Right. Remember to keep the party a surprise, okay?"

"I'll remember."

"Will needs to meet these people, Baby."

"I'm sure he does. Bye, Billy."

"Bye, honeybun. See you tomorrow night."

* * *

Clover was ready and waiting when Will rang her door-bell at seven the next evening. Billy's party would be casual dress, she knew, which fit her request for an informal dinner. Everything always seemed to work out for everyone else, but when was it going to work out for her?

Feeling just a tad sorry for herself, Clover opened the door. Instantly every feeling but awareness of Will Lang deserted her system in one massive swoop. He was gorgeous, wearing Western-cut pants and shirt in a luscious blue-gray color that seemed to intensify the blue of his eyes, and highly polished black boots. His dark, thick hair was becomingly tidy, but any woman within fifty yards would feel an urge to muss it.

She did, at any rate. And there, on his shirt again, were those pearlescent buttons with the concealed snaps. One quick jerk ... only one ...

Clover blinked and aligned her wayward thoughts. "Hi. Let me get my purse. I'm all ready."

"Beautiful and prompt, too," Will said with a grin. "Have you no faults at all, Miss Clover?"

She laughed. Will had a way about him that made her feel like laughing, and Lord he was handsome!

"Why, Mr. Lang, how you do ramble on and flatter a girl," she said in her best southern-belle drawl.

Will took her hand, bent over and planted a loud and smacking kiss just below her watch. "Frankly, my dear," he drawled, "I don't give a damn." Still bent over, he peered up at her. "That was the only line I could think of."

Clover giggled. "It was good enough." She withdrew her hand and darted into the foyer for her purse. Stepping outside, she closed the door. "Will, I need to drive by Billy's before we have dinner. Is that all right?"

"Sure, no problem."

Clover saw a silver BMW at the curb. "Is that yours?"

"Been mine for five years."

"I knew something was in the garage, but I never did see it."

"That's because I usually drive the pickup." Will opened the passenger door for Clover to get in, then walked around the front of the car and slid behind the wheel. "Just an old country boy at heart, I guess."

"A *genuine* country boy doesn't keep a classic BMW in his garage," Clover observed dryly. "Must be a little city somewhere among all that drawl and corn pone."

"Corn pone! Miss Clover, you cut, you stab, you wound!"

"Hogwash."

They looked at each other and laughed.

About half a mile away from her parents' home, Clover began to get uneasy. She'd told Billy the God's truth about disliking surprise parties. Did anyone really enjoy being taken by surprise?

She glanced at Will and *knew* that he would hate a bunch of strangers popping out of nowhere and yelling "Surprise!"

Of course, that image was probably exaggerated. Even Billy wouldn't stash people behind sofas and tables and behave as though Will should be thrilled at being taken unaware.

Or would he?

"What?" Will questioned, sensing Clover's unease. She looked terrific tonight in a pale pink dress and high-heeled pink sandals. Right at the moment, however, she also looked uncomfortable.

"Uh . . . Will, you and me . . . I mean . . . there's a lot we don't know about each other."

"True." What was she getting at?

"Well..." Clover faced front abruptly, muttering, "My loyalties are divided. I don't know what to do."

"Your loyalties are divided? I don't get it. What loyalties are you talking about?"

"If I were in your shoes, I'd want to know. I'd appreciate knowing, and I would thank the person who told me."

Will drove another block, then pulled the car over to the curb. He turned and laid his arm along the top of the seat. Whatever sexy scent Clover was wearing was wafting his way. He took a subtle sniff, suffered an intense jolt to his nervous system and forced a smile. "Tell me what, Clover?"

She had to tell him, Clover decided. A surprise party was ridiculous. Her head turned slightly, just enough to put Will in her line of vision. "Billy asked me to bring you back to the house tonight. He's giving a party—a surprise party—to introduce you to his friends."

Will stiffened.

Clover cleared her throat. "Say something."

"All right," Will said slowly. "I wish he weren't doing that."

"You do?"

"I don't mind meeting people, but..." Will drew a breath and began again. "I guess I do mind."

"Billy said they were people you should meet." Clover gnawed at the lipstick on her lower lip. "He's going to kill me for spilling the beans. Now do you understand why I mentioned divided loyalties?"

Will's tension relaxed into a smile, and he moved his hand from the seat back to Clover's hair. "You've pleased me. I'll act properly surprised, don't worry, but I won't ever forget that you counted me as one of your loyalties, Baby.''

Clover's eyes widened. She'd done precisely as Will had said without thinking of how it could look to him. Certainly loyalty to her father should supersede any she might feel for a man she'd only known a few weeks. Why, in heaven's name, would she feel loyalty to Will in the first place?

Logical or not, something had forced her into protecting Will against a nonsensical, completely unnecessary surprise.

And sitting in his car, with the sun going down and Will's fingertips grazing her hair, Clover knew that she was losing the battle to remain aloof from this music man.

It didn't make her happy. She might be falling in love, but the idea wasn't at all uplifting or elating. Rather, something sighed within her.

"Don't look so forlorn, honey. Billy will never know you told me, I promise."

"It's . . . not that," she whispered.

Will inched a little closer. "What is it, then?"

Clover practically wailed, "I like you."

Will peered at her in the semidarkness. "And that makes you unhappy?"

"I don't want to like anyone . . . a man, I mean." It was such a blatant lie, Clover marveled that her tongue didn't fall off. But it was the only thing she could think of to explain her ludicrous mood.

Other than the truth, which simply would not come out of her mouth. It never would, she suspected. Never would she have the nerve to look Will Lang in the eye and say straight out that she didn't want him playing in a band. He would think her demented. Her own vocation—haphazard as it was—centered on music. She'd grown up with music, took her first steps and then danced through her preschool years in time to her parents' guitars. Anyone in the Dove household lived and breathed music. She certainly hadn't been an exception.

But she was now; she had been for quite a few years.

All she was doing, she realized sadly, was perplexing Will. He was already looking at her as though he thought she might be a little light in the upper story. Further hedging would only amplify his confusion.

"We'd better go. Billy's probably on pins and needles waiting for you to arrive," she said.

"Do you know what I wish?" Will said. "I wish that I hadn't gotten a sudden attack of high-mindedness that day at Bear Creek. Before Billy and Francine showed up. You didn't have any hang-ups that day, Baby."

Clover cast her eyes downward. "I know."

"Even that night in the tent, with Billy and Francine right outside..."

"I know," she whispered.

"And now you wish you didn't like me." Will took her chin and brought her face up. "Look at me, Clover." Her eyes lifted. "I'm going to destroy every fear you have, if it's fear we're dealing with. Whatever it is, whatever's causing your unhappiness, I'm going to pulverize it into dust."

"You don't understand."

"You've got that right." Will's eyes searched hers. "The other night at your place I told myself to stay cool with you. But I don't feel cool. You're not feeling so cool, either, are you?"

"I'm not at all...cool."

"Oh, Baby," he whispered, and brought her forward in a sweeping embrace. His mouth sought hers and found it. She leaned into him and kissed him back. His lips felt like heaven on earth, and hers parted to permit a mating of their tongues.

Emotions exploded. They strained together, kissing hungrily, groping, attempting an impossible intimacy when they were so completely clothed and on the front seat of a car. Their legs and arms tangled. The skirt of Clover's dress got twisted up and around her thighs.

Why hadn't this happened in her condo? thought Will.

Why couldn't she stop this from happening? thought Clover.

And the kissing went on, until neither could breathe without gasps and Clover was just about to yank his shirt open.

Then they fell apart, their heads back against the seat, their lungs laboring for air.

"We've...got...to go," Clover stammered. "The party..."

The damned party. Will had a mind to skip the party completely, to drive back to Clover's condo and spend the night doing what they both wanted.

But he couldn't do that to Billy. He turned his head to see Clover. Her hair was disheveled, her lipstick smeared and she'd never looked more desirable. No woman had ever looked more desirable.

"Maybe we won't have to stay long," he mumbled thickly.

"Fat chance," Clover breathed.

"Yeah, you're probably right."

There was no probably about it, Clover knew. Billy's parties were a little odd by some people's standards. For one thing, beer was the only alcohol served, and not all that much of that. But there'd be lots of food and soft drinks, although good food was not what drew people to a Dove wingding. It was music. Anyone who played an instrument would have it with him, and the music would go on until the wee hours.

No, Will would not get away with only a brief appearance. The party was for him, and Billy would see to it that his guest of honor was right in the middle of as much hoopla as was possible to create in one evening.

Clover looked longingly at Will as he started the car, positive that he was muttering some rather impolite phrases under his breath. Her heart might never slow down and resume a normal beat, she thought. Her libido had finally grown up, apparently, and it wasn't going to calm down until Will Lang soothed it into submission.

Submission. What an unusual word for her to be using. But everything about this relationship was unusual. Every other one, the dates in her past, the parade of male acquaintances, had been as bland as plain yogurt. Will was a hot fudge sundae, the richest, most caloric and full-of-cholesterol sweet-treat imaginable. Tempting but dangerous.

During the remaining short drive, Clover hastily repaired her lipstick and brushed her hair. Arriving at her parents' home, she smiled wryly. There were no strange cars in sight; it was, indeed, going to be a surprise party.

Will cut the engine and looked at her. Clover mustered up a weak smile. "Later," Will said softly.

She sighed, because "later" in this instance might not be until dawn.

The party was in full swing. The Dove residence was large and sprawling, and groups filled the enormous family room, the music room and the living room. Will had been introduced to so many people, he couldn't possibly remember all their names. Not everyone was a stranger, he'd discovered. There were a lot of old-timers, people he'd known through his father.

And then someone had pressed a guitar into his hands, and he'd been urged along to the music room. The faces and talent on the "stage" changed every so often, but the music only stopped long enough to dampen dry throats or to discuss a song someone wanted to try.

Clover wandered from room to room and mingled, saying hello and chatting with the guests. Everyone seemed to have something good to say about Will. "He's Pudge's son, all right." "Good-looking fellow." "He sure can make that guitar sing."

With a plate of food, Clover found a reasonably quiet corner and sat down to eat. Lord knew when Will would find the time. He was the man of the evening, no question about it.

And, sad as it was for Clover to face, he fit in. His great personality, his good looks and his marvelous talent made him perfect for this crowd. He even appeared to be enjoying the affair. Immensely.

Clover sighed and bit into a shrimp-stuffed mushroom. A young woman carrying a plate walked up. "Hi. Mind if I join you?"

"Please do."

"Thanks." The woman moved a chair closer and sat down. With her plate on her lap, she offered her hand. "I'm Sara Green."

Clover hoped her surprise didn't show. "I'm Clover Dove."

"I know." They shook hands. "Billy talks about you so much, I've been anxious to meet you."

It was sinking into Clover's brain that Sara Green was in her mother's house when Francine was out of town. Clover didn't want to view the situation with any negative aspects, but her system was absorbing Sara's pretty face, soft brown, simply styled hair and chocolate-brown eyes, with a touch of resentment. Francine and Billy were close again, and this young woman could cause an explosion that might never settle down.

And yet, there wasn't so much as a hint of deceit or treachery on Sara Green's face. "Nice party," she commented. "Great food."

"Yes," Clover responded automatically, acutely conscious of Sara's expressions. "Billy invites everyone he knows to his shindigs."

Sara laughed pleasantly. "Billy's wonderful. But then, I'm sure I don't have to tell you that."

Clover cleared her throat. "Have you met Francine?"

Sara shook her head. "Not yet." She smiled. "I'm going on Billy's next tour, you know."

"How . . . nice." Sara Green and Billy and . . . Will. Clover's heart sank clear to her knees.

"It's a lot more than nice, Clover. Billy's really helped with my career. I can't praise Billy Dove enough. He's a kindhearted, generous man."

"He's . . . yes, he's generous and kind." And good-looking and famous and rich. Did those things matter to Sara? Was her admiration of Billy Dove really only confined to gratitude that he'd nudged her career along?

Clover despised jealousy, but entertainers drew the opposite sex the way wildflowers drew bees. Her mother and father had lived with this sort of thing their entire lives. And if Will stayed in the music business, women by the droves would be doing stupid things such as passing him their room keys, and chasing after him like mindless, drooling idiots.

The plate of delicious tidbits on Clover's lap had been barely touched, but her appetite had disappeared in a maelstrom of confused emotions.

She got up. "Sara, it was nice meeting you, but I just thought of something I have to do."

"Oh?"

"An appointment that slipped my mind," Clover mumbled. "We'll see each other again, I'm sure. Bye for now."

Clover hurried off, deserted her plate of food by placing it on a table and wound through the crowd to find her father. He was, surprisingly, in the kitchen alone, icing down a tub of soft drinks and beer.

He looked up. "Hi, Baby. Having a good time?"

"Billy, I have to go. Will's busy, so would you tell him that I had to leave?"

Billy had been bent over, and he straightened up from his task. "How come? The party's just getting started."

"I know, and it's a wonderful party. But I really do have to go."

"Well, heck!"

"I'm sorry."

"Didn't you come with Will? How're you gonna leave?"

Good question. "Uh...maybe I could borrow one of your cars?"

"Well, sure, but—"

Clover dropped a quick kiss on her father's cheek. "Thanks. I'll talk to you soon. Which car should I use?"

"You know where the keys are. Take any one of them you want. Clover...this don't make sense."

"No, it doesn't. None of it makes sense. And maybe that's what I'm trying to figure out. Don't worry, okay? I'll call you tomorrow."

Escaping the crowded house felt like a release from oppression for Clover. Breathing more freely, she walked to the garage and got into Billy's Wagoneer.

But she was barely out of the long driveway before the tears started.

She wanted a farm. She wanted to get completely away from guitars and singers and fiddle players, totally away from anyone and everyone even remotely connected with the music business.

Will was playing and laughing and having a great old time. Sara Green was in her mother's house. She didn't know what Billy was doing. It might be nothing more than Sara had said, helping her with her career.

But it all hurt. Dammit, it hurt!

And if she didn't stay away from Will Lang, she was going to hurt a hell of a lot more than she did right now!

Nine

During the drive home Clover worried about how Will might feel when he learned that she'd left the party. Letting him know would have been considerate, which she would have gladly done under ordinary circumstances.

But circumstances weren't at all ordinary. What she would like to do, Clover realized uneasily, was avoid Will for a while. Give him the chance to make up his mind about his new career without her or anyone else's input. Her staying out of it wouldn't assure Will of a completely unbiased decision, of course. Billy and many other musicians would be in there touting the good points of the music business.

And there were many good points; even Clover couldn't say there weren't.

It was just that it wasn't for her, and neither was a man who seemed to be getting more involved in it every day.

Clover parked the Wagoneer in front of her condo, took the keys and went inside. She walked directly to the telephone and dialed a long-distance number. A woman answered.

"Shelley? Clover Dove. How are you?"

"Well, for heaven's sake! I was just thinking about you a little while ago. What've you got, ESP?"

"Not even close, Shelley. Actually I need a place to hide out for about a week."

"Hide out! What'd you do, rob a bank?"

"I'll tell you all about it if you invite me for a visit."

"You've got it! I'll be thrilled to see you. When are you coming?"

"Is tonight too soon?"

"My, you *are* in a hurry. Well, come along, Clover. I'll be watching for you."

"Thanks, Shelley. See you in about . . . how long should it take me to drive there?"

"About three hours. Are you sure you can find Shamrock?"

"I know exactly how to get there. I just wasn't sure of the distance. See you soon."

Shelley Dunn had gone to school with Clover, and had recently moved from Nashville to Shamrock, a little town on the edge of a small lake. Shelley had a sad history. She'd married and lost her husband, Paul Dunn, to a highway accident, all within two years. Clover had stayed in touch with her old friend after her move, but so far hadn't visited her.

Now was a propitious time. She would stay with Shelley until after Billy took his band on tour. They would be gone for several weeks, and when Will returned he would have a better idea of whether or not the music business was going to be a permanent part of his future.

It was too bad that Will would have to wade through knee-deep bragging and boasting from the other band members, and there was Billy's influence to combat, as well. Maybe Will didn't even realize that there was a decision to make, but Clover believed there was, and if he chose performing over his previous simple life-style, there was very little chance for the two of them.

But what if he came back disenchanted?

Clover was reluctant to plan that far ahead. Quickly she packed a suitcase and made a few calls so her friends and working associates wouldn't notify the police that she'd disappeared. One of them promised to contact Billy in the morning and let him know that Clover was fine but out of Nashville for an indefinite period.

Will would just have to hear it secondhand. Clover couldn't risk talking to Will just now.

Clover returned home after a pleasant week in Shamrock. She had poured out the whole story to Shelley, who had listened without comment until Clover wound down.

Then she had offered some advice. *"Sounds to me like you're in love with Will Lang, Clover. Let me say this. As short a time as Paul and I had together, I wouldn't trade it for anything else in the world. Think real hard before you leap in any direction, my friend. People don't fall in love every day. Real love is a rarity and immeasurably valuable."*

Clover believed her friend. Real love *was* immeasurably valuable. But there was still one fly in the ointment of that lovely philosophy: Billy and Francine's stormy relationship. They were in love with each other, but were they happy?

Will was on tour right now—along with attractive women like Sara Green and a countless number of female

fans. Some performers' heads were turned by adulation
and they tumbled into a different bed every night. Some
couldn't handle the pressure coming at them from all directions and sought solace in alcohol or drugs. Only the
strong survived success in the entertainment world. Success was sometimes more difficult to deal with than fail-
ure.

Clover was certain of one thing: Will would get an ed-
ucation. What he would do with it was anybody's guess,
and she could only hope that he was as levelheaded as Billy
proclaimed.

From her own personal point of view, she was crazy
about Will. The in-depth discussions with Shelley had
clarified her feelings in that respect, and she was glad that
she'd left Nashville when she had.

Of course, nothing was settled. Admitting intense feelings for Will didn't assure a serene future. What if he
stayed in the music business?

Clover knew that she was hoping Will would hate it. She
fantasized a scene where he walked in and announced a
total and permanent break with professional entertaining.
Never would she expect him to give up music entirely; he
was too good to never pick up a guitar again.

But in the fantasy, after he told her about quitting the
business, they would talk about loving each other, and they
would make love and make plans. It was a dream, yes, but
it wasn't one that was impossible to attain.

It all hinged on Will.

The first call Clover made upon her return was to her
parents' home. She got their blasted answering machine,
which destroyed her hope of immediately speaking to
Francine. Not that Clover was positive that Francine was
back from her tour. There were times when both Billy and

Francine were away from Nashville, each with their own groups and in different parts of the country.

Clover had turned off her own answering machine before leaving town, so there wasn't a stack of messages awaiting her. In fact, the condo felt eerily empty and she felt strangely disconnected.

It was an odd sensation, one she'd never noticed before. She'd only been gone a week, certainly not long enough to feel as if everyone she knew had vanished.

But everyone important *had* vanished—her mother, her father and ... Will.

Where was he? In what city, what state?

Clover threw herself on the sofa, folded her arms and frowned. Maybe she shouldn't have gone off so hastily. Talking to Shelley had been good therapy, but knowing where Will was right now would be immensely comforting.

The phone rang, and Clover nearly tripped over herself getting off the couch and running to answer it. "Hello?"

"Well, for pete's sake!" Francine said into her ear. "Where in heck have you been? I've been trying to get hold of you for days. Honestly, Clover—"

"Mother, please! I only went to Shamrock to see Shelley Dunn."

"Well, you might have told someone. There wasn't a note in the house when I got home, not a hint. Did your father know where you went?"

"Uh ... no."

"Clover, don't you ever do that again! I'm ten years older today than I was yesterday, and if there's anything I don't need, it's premature old age! Just wait until you have children, young woman, you'll find out that a mother doesn't stop worrying just because her daughter's an adult."

Clover felt about two inches high. "I'm sorry. You were gone, and I asked Maddie Sumner to contact Billy and let him know I'd be away for a while. I'm sorry he didn't leave you a note or something."

"Well...I'm sorry, too. I shouldn't have lit into you, but I really was worried, Baby. You've never gone off like that before. I hate coming home to an empty house, anyway. Billy's on tour, and..."

Clover heard a choking sound. "Mother, are you crying?"

"No, but I feel like it."

"Billy hasn't called?"

"He got the answering machine. Said he'd call again this evening."

"Will's on tour with him," Clover said quietly, then waited through a long stretch of silence. "Francine?"

"Will's important to you, isn't he?"

Clover sighed. "Yes."

"Does he know?"

"I...doubt it."

"Does your father know?"

"No, of course not."

"You've kept it all to yourself. Why, Baby? Why didn't you let Will know how you feel?"

Clover twisted the telephone cord with her right hand. "I didn't really know myself until recently. Mother, please don't say anything to anyone about it, okay?"

"Who would I tell, the cleaning lady?"

Clover smiled at the wry sarcasm in Francine's naturally husky voice. "I can't tell Will what to do with his life, Mother."

"Meaning?"

"Meaning, he can do whatever he wants."

"Clover, did you and Will argue about him going on that tour?"

"Argue! Of course not. We never even discussed it."

"But that's what this is all about, isn't it?"

"I suppose," Clover concurred. "Just don't say anything, okay? When Will gets back...well, we'll see what happens."

"I guess that's wise," Francine said slowly.

"It's really all I can do," Clover said.

"Yes, I suppose it is. Not to change the subject, but how is Shelley doing?"

Clover related that Shelley was getting her life together, and mother and daughter chatted about this and that for a good half hour.

Finally Francine said that she had a million things to do and had better get off the phone. Clover hung up feeling much more stable and put herself to work unpacking her suitcase.

Will was stretched out, fully clothed, on the bed in his hotel room. The Dove band was presently between a 4:00 p.m. and an 8:00 p.m. show. A couple of the band members were downstairs in the hotel lounge, however, Will had refused an invitation to join them.

Someone knocked at the door. "Come on in," Will called. "It's open."

Billy walked in. "Sleeping?"

Will sat up and put his feet on the floor. "Thinking."

"Just talked to Francine," Billy said as he chose a chair and sat down.

"How is she?"

"Um...fine, fine. She said that Clover got home."

Will cocked an eyebrow. He was pretty ticked off at Clover for leaving Billy's party the way she had. And then, when he'd tried to call her, even her damned answering machine hadn't been working. He'd left the party and gone to her empty condo. It was the next day that Billy told him she'd taken some sort of trip. Just like that, without one word to anyone, she'd taken a trip.

He didn't understand Miss Clover. She melted when he kissed her then ran off when he wasn't looking. How was a man to figure out a woman who behaved so erratically?

Billy stuck his legs straight out in front of the chair and stared at his boots. "Uh, Will, how do you like the tour?"

Will sobered. The tour was, in fact, getting him down. But his attitude contained a great deal of ambivalence. He wondered how much Billy depended on him, and how Clover might feel about him quitting before really giving the business a fair trial. He didn't want to do anything hasty, so he only said quietly, "I'm not much for crowds and strange hotel rooms, Billy."

"Figured that. Not too many of us get anything out of the traveling. But there's a lot more to the music business than tourin'. When we get back to Nashville, we'll be working on putting out a new album and making a few videos. We perform at the Opry quite a bit, too."

"Yeah, I know," Will said with a slight nod of his head. "There's some real good aspects to the business, no question about it."

"You don't need the money."

"No, I don't need the money." Will leveled a gaze on Billy. "I don't need the applause, either, Billy. Pa did, but I don't."

Billy's eyes gentled in internal circumspection. "I miss old Pudge. He was a fine man, Will, the best."

"He was like you, Billy, a straight-shooter."

Billy cleared his throat. "Yeah, well, I don't always shoot so straight. I didn't tell Francine that Sara Green is on the tour. I been worried about that, but heck, Sara is a good singer, Will, and Frannie would only throw a fit if she knew.''

"Sara's a comer, Billy. She's going to be a big star.''

"Yeah, she is. But she don't mean anything to me personally. Know what I mean?''

"Yes.''

Billy uncoiled his lanky frame and stood up. ''Well, I only stopped by for a minute. I'm gonna go lie down and catch a nap.''

Will got up. ''Sure, Billy, you do that.''

After Billy had gone, Will sat on the bed again. The phone was right on the bed stand and Clover was home. Why in heck had she gone off that way? What was he to think about such blatant inconsideration? Did she care what he thought?

Maybe not. But if he meant nothing to her, why did she respond to his every advance?

When he thought of Clover, his insides felt peculiar, as if they'd gotten sort of mushy. The sensation was both good and bad, sometimes making him grit his teeth in frustration, other times making him silly and sentimental. Whatever its cause and effect, he'd learned that it wasn't going to go away.

What in heck was he doing so far from home? What he'd like to do was talk to Clover and find out how she truly felt about the direction his life was taking.

But was it fair to lay his uncertainty on her?

Besides, if she had any negative feelings on the matter, wouldn't she have already said so? No, he couldn't burden Clover with a decision only he should make.

But he still wanted to talk to her. Picking up the phone, Will punched out Clover's number, which he now knew by heart. Her phone rang once, twice, a third time.

Then he heard, "Hello?"

He leaned back against the headboard and said in a low, mellow voice, "Hi, Baby."

In her condo, holding the phone, Clover's heart nearly stopped. "Will! Hi, how are you?"

He was determined not to mention her rude departure, or anything else that might widen the breach between them. "I'm doing great. How're you doing?"

Clover felt like a heavy weight had just descended upon her head. He was doing great? "Uh...I'm doing great, too. Had a nice visit with an old friend."

"Apparently you went out of town."

"Shelley lives in Shamrock. Have you ever been there?"

"I think so, a few years back. Little town on a pretty lake?"

"That's it. Shelley lost her husband..." Clover talked about her friend for a few minutes. "Anyway, it was time I went to see her."

She waited for some sort of derogatory comment regarding her abrupt departure, but Will only said, "Sounds like it. Bet she was glad you came."

"Yes, she was." Wasn't he even a little put out about her unscheduled trip? "How's the tour going?"

"Billy's happy about it. We're playing to packed houses every show."

"That's good."

"We're going to Wichita, Kansas, tomorrow. I'm in my hotel room right now. We've got another show to do at eight o'clock." Will took a breath. "I miss you, Baby."

Tears suddenly burned Clover's eyes. "I miss you, too, Will."

"Can I call you again tomorrow?"

The tears dripped down Clover's cheeks. "Please do."

"I'm not sure about the time. Probably late afternoon."

"I'll be here."

"When I get back..."

"Yes, Will? When you get back?"

He had no ready reply. When he got back what? Good question, *very* good question. There seemed to be an awful lot they didn't, or couldn't, say to each other.

But he *could* let her know that he cared. "I wish we were together right now," he said raggedly. The mush in his body was solidifying, particularly in one significant area.

"Do you?" she whispered, suddenly struck with an almost painful attack of aches and hot flushes. If they were together right now, they would make love. *She* would insist on it, by damn! She would rip those snaps on his shirt open and then go for his belt buckle.

The image weakened her knees, and Will's next comment didn't help her condition. "If we were, if you were here or I was there...oh, Baby, I want you. Just the sound of your voice is driving me nuts."

It didn't matter, Clover realized sadly. It didn't matter if he played music or dug ditches. It didn't matter if he walked on his feet or his hands. Nothing mattered. She wanted him, she loved him.

She'd done her best, she'd tried everything she could think of to change the course of events. But fate, or some darned thing, had destined her to fall in love with Will Lang, and that's precisely where she was at—deeply, abidingly in love with a music man.

"I want you, too," she said huskily.

"You've fought it."

"Yes," she concurred without explanation. "I'm not fighting it any longer."

"I have to finish the tour."

"I know you do."

"But I'll see you the minute I get back."

"I'll be waiting."

Clover couldn't say that she slept any better that night, because she tossed and turned at regular intervals.

But her restlessness was purely physical; it wasn't possible to sleep soundly with so much desire running wild in her system. When Will got back...

Dear God, when Will got back they were going to...

Yes...again and again.

She closed her eyes against the tears. She loved him, and if he wanted to play in a band for the rest of his life, she would endure.

Somehow.

Ten

――――――

Will called every day. A few times Clover was away from the condo at the crucial moment and missed his calls, but most days she was there to take them.

They talked and talked. About childhood and growing up, about the schools they'd attended and the friends they'd made along the way. About Clover's charity work and Will's cabinetmaking. They talked about Nashville and politics and cars, about the evening news and articles each had read in the newspapers. About favorite magazines, movies, books, comedians, actors. They told jokes and laughed together.

They covered almost every imaginable subject during those wonderful long-distance conversations, with one notable exception. Music.

What was strange for Clover was that she couldn't detect any evasion from Will about music. She didn't bring it up on purpose, but in his case, he just didn't seem interested.

Oh, yes, they didn't talk about love, either. Perhaps it didn't feel right to bring up such a monumentally important subject as love on the phone. Clover knew she deliberately avoided mentioning the word, and Will seemed to be doing the same. It was in the back of her mind, though, almost constantly. She liked Will Lang so much, his voice, his outlook on life in general, and she liked the shivery little tingles in her own body because he was on the other end of the line.

Occasionally impatience would enter their conversation. The days were going by quickly, but not quickly enough.

And then Will said one evening, "I'll be home in two days."

The next night he told her that he'd see her the following evening. "We should be back in Nashville around 10:00 p.m. Will you still be up?"

"I'll be up. Come right over."

All the next day Clover thought about Will. While she tended to some errands and spent three hours at the children's home, Will was uppermost in her mind.

She arrived home around six-thirty in a flurry of anticipation and anxiety. Her stomach was so jumpy with butterflies, eating solid food was impossible, so she warmed a bowl of soup for dinner and barely touched that.

Her bath took up an hour, her hair and makeup another forty minutes. By nine she was bathed, shampooed and blow-dried, made-up, dressed and pacing. She slowed down long enough to apply another coat of polish to her manicure, then walked around waving her hands and blowing on her nails to dry them.

If my heart beats any harder, it will burst through my chest!

She straightened a pillow on the sofa, aligned a picture on the wall, looked out the window, stared at the phone, ate a cracker then dashed back to the bathroom to brush her teeth again. Which required freshening her lipstick.

Did I use too much perfume?

Or not enough.

The CD player was turned on and adjusted at least a dozen times. Lamps were switched on and off and then on again. She wanted everything perfect.

What in God's name will we say to each other?

Never had she been in such a tizzy. One second she was soaring, the next scared out of her mind.

Darkness had descended. The lamps were necessary and no longer merely a romantic prop.

Was her dress right? She'd chosen a simple, loosely structured white dress and white sandals. Maybe she should put on something fancier. High heels.

Oh, damn.

At ten-fifteen the phone rang. She rushed to answer it, positive that Will was in town and calling to let her know.

It was her mother.

"Oh, hi," she said, unable to keep her disappointment from showing.

"Billy called. The bus broke down about eighty miles east of the city. They're in a small town and everything is closed up tight. They won't be home until tomorrow."

If a giant pin had suddenly pricked her skin and let all the air out of Clover, she couldn't have been more deflated.

"Baby?"

"I'm here," Clover said in a low voice.

"Were you expecting to see Will tonight?"

Clover lifted her chin. "I invited him, Mother."

"I see. It's getting serious between you and Will, isn't it?"

"We've done a lot of talking on the phone."

"Clover, I know you don't like what your father and I do for a living. What if Will does the same thing?"

"Mother, it isn't that I don't like it—"

"Maybe I didn't use the best words, but you know what I mean."

"Yes," Clover said softly. "I know what you mean. I'm sorry. I can't help the way I feel."

"Don't apologize. You're entitled to your opinion."

"I'm not sure that's true where you and Billy are concerned. You've both been good parents, and a daughter really has no right to judge decisions made by her mother and father before she was even born."

"You have a point."

"What I do have a right to judge, Mother, is the career of any man I . . ." Clover's voice trailed off.

"Love? Hope to marry?"

"And maybe judge isn't the best word, either," Clover said quickly, ignoring Francine's reference to disturbing topics. "I'm not judging Will, or I'm trying very hard not to, but tonight is a good example of the music business. Itineraries are only so much paper, aren't they?"

"They're reliable unless something unexpected occurs. No one could predict engine trouble with the bus, Clover."

"True, but..." Clover stopped and sighed. "I feel petty for even mentioning it, and I'm certainly not going to say anything to Will about it when he gets here."

"You're not going to let him know that you'd rather he quit the band? Clover, I'm not sure that's wise."

"It's the way I want it, Mother."

Francine sighed. "If you say so."

"Maybe Will's trying to call me. Would you mind if we said goodbye?"

"No, I don't mind."

Clover stayed up until midnight. There had to be an available phone in that little town or Billy wouldn't have been able to call Francine, but Will didn't call. Yawning, Clover finally undressed, donned a thigh-length nightie and crawled into bed.

A bell was ringing. Over and over again. Clover struggled out of a deep sleep and groggily wondered if it was the phone or the doorbell.

It pealed again. Someone was laying on the doorbell.

Squinty-eyed and a little irritated, Clover got out of bed and found a robe. Tying the sash as she went, she made her way through the dark rooms to the front door. At the last minute, just barely clearheaded enough to remember that it was the middle of the night, she snapped on the outside light and peeked through the peephole.

"Will!" Suddenly awkward with haste, Clover fumbled with the dead bolt and threw the door open. "How in the world..."

He stepped forward and pulled her into his arms. Wrapping her arms around his waist, she snuggled against him. "Oh, Will."

His breath heated her hair. "I woke people up in that little town until I found someone who would drive me to Nashville."

Clover laughed. "Did you really?"

"I told you I'd be here."

"So you did. I stayed up until midnight. What time is it now?"

"Around one-thirty. My things are on your stoop. I just had the guy drop me off, suitcases and all." Will cupped the back of her head and looked at her. "I can't believe we're finally together. Let me kiss you, Miss Clover."

His lips descended to hers. Something warm and alive sprouted in Clover. Will's mouth tasted minty, his clothing smelled of nighttime dampness. She stood on tiptoe and wound her arms around his neck, locking her hands together just above his shirt collar.

"Ah," Will murmured. The exhaustion he'd arrived with was fading fast. He felt, in fact, as if he'd come home. And he was standing in Clover's foyer, which didn't even slightly resemble his own house.

But it was the woman in his arms that felt like home, not the surroundings.

He stroked her back. "Shall I bring in my things?"

"Uh . . . yes. Yes, of course." Obviously he planned to spend the remainder of the night in her condo, and the mere thought made her heart pound.

But wasn't that what she'd been waiting for? He'd said it plainly on the phone, and so had she—they wanted each other.

Still, he caught the faint note of reluctance in her voice. "Only if you're sure, honey," he said softly. The outside light reflected in his eyes. He smiled after a moment. "Let me get my things so we can close the door."

He brought in his luggage and set it down on the parquet floor. Clover nervously tightened the sash at her waist. "Are you hungry?"

He wasn't, but there was tension between them that he hadn't anticipated. Long talks on the telephone, as lively and informative as they'd been, were apparently poor substitutes for face-to-face interaction. "A little," he lied.

Clover relaxed and began snapping on lights. "The refrigerator's full. I'll make you a sandwich."

"Thanks." Will followed her to the kitchen. She looked so beautiful he couldn't stop staring. Hair mussed, no makeup, clean, shiny skin, shapeless robe; he liked every detail of her appearance. Clover was akin to his own right arm, he realized, a very important part of Will Lang. She was that special woman he'd always suspected was out there.

"Turkey or beef?" Clover questioned from the open refrigerator.

"Beef."

"And lettuce and tomato?"

"Fine."

Clover took the sandwich ingredients from the fridge to the counter. "Francine called to tell me about the bus breaking down," she said with her back to Will.

"Were you disappointed?"

He'd spoken so softly that prickles danced up Clover's spine. "Very," she huskily admitted after a pause, and glanced at him over her shoulder. "I wondered if you would call."

He couldn't continue with pretense. Some of their phone conversations had been rather graphic, and they both knew why he was here. "Clover, I don't want a sandwich."

"You don't?"

He didn't answer, just looked at her for the longest time. A flush crept up her throat and face. But she couldn't deflect her gaze, and she realized that his mind was not at all on food, although there was unquestionable hunger in his expression.

With a runaway heartbeat, she began putting the food away. When everything was back in the refrigerator, she took a deep breath and faced him. Without a word she walked over to where he was standing and lifted her eyes to his.

"I'm very glad you found someone to drive you here," she said, and raised a hand and laid it on his chest.

Will raised his own hand and covered hers. "You look so young in that robe," he said huskily. "I'm thinking that you look like a little girl, but you're not a little girl, are you? You're a grown woman, and you were waiting for me."

"Yes, I was," she said softly. "And now you're here."

"All the times we talked on the phone I was thinking of this, of being with you and touching you." Will brushed a lock of her hair back from her forehead. "Touching you goes right through me, Baby, like an electrical current. Do you feel it?"

God, yes, she felt it. Her senses were seared by it. Describing the sensation as an electrical current was only partially accurate, because one didn't stand near an electrical outlet and hope for a string of shocks. Yet there *was* something electrifying about the jolting desire in her system.

"I feel something very powerful," she whispered.

Will lifted her hand from his chest to his lips and kissed her fingertips, one by one. "Powerful...yes. We get along, don't we?"

"In many ways."

Will slowly smiled, cupped her face with his hands and lowered his head. His lips touched hers gently, then began taking nipping little kisses. "Sweet . . . so sweet," he whispered.

Clover's heart was racing. She closed her eyes to marvel at the sensations rocketing through her body. Feelings that had never been so acute before—desire, pleasure, yearning.

And then they were in each other's arms, body straining against body. They clung and rocked together, kissing each other with needful gasps. Will's hands skimmed down the back of Clover's robe, while mindlessly she tore his shirt open.

The snaps gave, as she'd envisioned they would. His chest was bare, as she'd seen it in her fantasies. She pressed her lips to the heated skin between the panels of his shirt, whispering, "I've dreamed of this."

Her passion pleased Will tremendously. It was how he'd been thinking of her—free spirited, passionate, uninhibited.

And without clothing. With nothing at all between his hands and her bare skin.

He untied the sash of her robe and pushed the garment from her shoulders. It fell in a puddle of blue terry at her feet. Her short gown was made of something silky and slippery. It excited him, and he ran his hands over it, absorbing the lush female curves beneath it.

But it took only a few seconds for him to realize that she wore nothing beneath it. An intense wave of desire nearly blinded him. He lifted the gown's hem and stroked the rounded swells of her behind. Their kisses were becoming greedy, impatient. Clover was trying to undo his belt buckle, which was no easy feat when neither of them was standing still.

Will stopped everything else going on by catching her into a fierce embrace. He'd been patient for so long. He'd barely looked at other women, and certainly not with anything resembling what he felt for Clover. These days, he couldn't even imagine wanting another woman.

"Oh, Baby," he whispered raggedly. "I'm yours. Don't ever doubt it."

With those words, any stray remnants of doubt tucked into the far reaches of Clover's mind vanished. She kissed his mouth, a long, lingering mating of lips and tongues that deteriorated her strength to the point of weakness.

"My room," she whispered.

Light-headed and soaring, Will scooped her up off the floor and into his arms. She laughed softly and burrowed her face into the inviting nook of his throat and shoulder. His strides were long and purposeful. "Which door?" he questioned in the hall.

"Last on the right." Being carried made her feel dizzy and slightly giggly. She hadn't pictured Will so eager and impetuous as to carry her to the bedroom.

She'd turned no lamps on in that room, and only diffused rays from the condo's other lights reached inside. The pale sheen through the doorway created a shadowy, almost ethereal atmosphere. Her bed, with its disheveled sheets and blankets, was little more than a silhouette.

"Can we have a light?" Will questioned while letting her feet slide to the floor. He kissed her before she could answer, and Clover immediately forgot the question.

So did Will. She was in his arms, warm and silky soft and smelling like no woman he'd ever known. His heartbeat was like a tom-tom in his chest. He wanted her with a desperation he'd never experienced before. He had protection with him, since he'd known they would make love. His mind catapulted from one thought to another. He knew that they had a future together, that what was happening to them was not trivial.

They were so in tune that their clothing disappeared without awkwardness. Naked, they tumbled to the bed and instantly intertwined legs and arms. They touched each other and explored feverish skin, kissing all the while.

Breathing and whispered endearments were accomplished with small gasps and moans.

Will wanted her with him all the way, wanted her pleasure more than his own. Besides, he wasn't seeking only pleasure from Clover. The internal force driving him demanded communion, a meshing and melding of spirits, his and hers. Branding her as his, claiming her as his, might be concepts too brash to mention, but they were in the back of his mind.

Her bare skin scorched the palms of his hands. He dipped his head to kiss her breasts, and then the flat, smooth plane of her belly. His kisses went lower, to each of her hipbones, to her thighs, to the soft mound of hair at their juncture. Each spot he kissed belonged to him now; he was staking his claim.

But so was Clover, if with entirely different thoughts. Her mind was dreamily overheated. Will's textures were marvelous, even if explored with some shyness. His skin was smooth in places, hair-roughened in others. And beneath it, his muscles rippled in a completely bewitching manner.

At moments a bit of worry filtered through the utter delight she was feeling, worry about Will's reaction to her virginity. Would he think it a gift or a hindrance? How, really, did men feel about chastity these days? Should she mention it beforehand, or let him discover it on his own?

He kissed his way up her body and sought her lips again. She held his face and put her heart and soul into a kiss that went on and on, dizzying her mind and eradicating all traces of worry. What would be, would be. He was her first man and had every chance of being her one and only. She could not even imagine another man in her bed like this.

Nearly delirious with desire, her head moved on the pillow. "Will . . . oh, Will."

"Baby..." His hand skimmed downward and probed gently between her thighs.

She gasped at the contact, but relaxed her legs and let them fall open. Her response was beyond her control, a rising passion that astonished her, a pleasure that was almost bittersweet with its nuances of wanting. She felt a strange selfishness derived from the knowledge that if he stopped, she might shrivel and die, or at the very least, hurt terribly for the rest of her days.

There were no virginal inhibitions remaining in her system. She wanted him in every way possible, wanted to make him hers, needed to show him that he *was* hers. And that she was his. Her hands became bold and wanton, and while he caressed and teased her most sensitive spot, she reached for his.

He groaned deep in his chest. Her hands were taking him to the brink much too quickly. His control was being pushed to the limits as it was; he couldn't wait any longer.

"Just a second, sweetheart," he whispered thickly, and moved to the edge of the bed to feel around for his jeans.

Initially surprised, Clover blinked, but it only took a moment for her to realize what he was doing, and she thanked God that one of them had some sense. She wasn't ignorant of necessities or what was only wise, but she honestly hadn't thought of birth control.

How lax of her. Did she *want* to get pregnant?

Frowning slightly, aware of a darting confusion, she was relieved when Will returned to hold her. His kisses were hot and agitated, more urgent than they'd been. Her confusion faded in a tide of renewed desire. Deep in her belly a spot of heat demanded and taunted. It pushed her deeper into his arms, drove her to seek a closer union with his body.

Breathing was difficult. There seemed to be pinpricks of light behind her eyes and a thrumming energy filling her cells and following the maze of nerves in her system.

Her voice was barely recognizable as her own. "Make love to me. I need you . . . I need . . ."

"I need, too, Baby," Will whispered, gladly moving into position. He joined them intimately and thrust for the final union.

Then he stopped, stunned by what he was feeling. For a moment his mind spun and words eluded him. Clover laid beneath him, looking pale in the dim light. "I didn't know," he finally whispered.

"How could you?" She touched his cheek with a hand. "Does it matter?"

Nearly overcome by emotion, Will could hardly speak. "It matters. It matters more than I can say."

But she could tell that he meant something wonderful, and her soul soared. "Don't let it stop you," she whispered. "Please."

His heart was thudding unmercifully. No woman could ever be as special to him as Clover was. That she was giving him the most precious gift a woman could give a man touched him in a way nothing else ever could have. No other man knew the joys and secrets of her body. She truly was his.

Tears blurred his vision. "I'll be gentle."

For the first time Clover felt more powerful than he. "Be whatever you are, whatever you feel."

"I don't want to hurt you."

She pulled his head down and kissed him, feeling his response and her own. They weren't two people at the moment, they were one. "Make love to me, Will Lang. Make me a woman," she whispered against his lips.

The blood in his body surged with a crazy leap of his heart. "Oh, Baby," he said hoarsely. "You make me fly."

"Make me fly, too, Will." She wrapped her legs around his hips, a purely instinctive invitation.

He knew the first plunge would cause her discomfort, but she knew it as well and neither of them wanted to get off of Clover's bed without fulfillment.

That's what he would give her, he thought. Her gift was precious, but so would his be valuable.

He moved gingerly, feeling his way. Then there was only one way, and he had to take it. She cried out, and he kissed her. "Shh, shh," he murmured. "The hurting's all over. Relax as much as you can."

She was trembling. Every woman had to go through it, but knowing the facts of life didn't quite prepare one for the tearing pain. Tears were stingingly close, but the last thing she wanted to do right now was cry.

Will kissed and soothed her. The memory of discomfort seemed to pass very quickly, almost as if it had happened a very long time ago. Maybe because the heat hadn't deserted her body after that one stab of pain...or maybe it was because Will was in her and magnificently aroused.

Clover felt more womanly than she ever had. And strangely generous. Expansive. As if she wanted to give and give to this incredible man.

Oddly she sensed from him the same generosity and desire to give.

His kisses moved over her face and, very gently, he made a sliding motion with his hips. Clover dampened her lips. Her eyes closed as pleasure blossomed in her most private places. How lovely, she thought. How mysterious.

Those first seedlings of pleasure weren't enough after a very short time, however. Her lips parted for air as a need for more pleasure gripped her senses.

Will was taking it easy, keeping a lid on his own emotions through sheer willpower. When her hips began to undulate with his, to rise to meet him, he nearly went over the edge. He felt her hands on his back, stroking, moving up and down restlessly.

Her virginity was utterly astonishing. Not that he'd thought her promiscuous, good Lord, no. But there was an enormous scale between promiscuity and virginity, and Clover was twenty-six years old. In this age of relaxed morality, what man even hoped for virginity in the woman he cared for?

More than cared for. He intended to spend the rest of his life with this beautiful, sensitive, sexy woman.

Dare he say so? Even at this most intimate of moments?

He gritted his teeth. Things weren't quite right in his life yet. There would be plenty of time to talk about the future, after he made a few adjustments. When he asked Clover to marry him, he wanted everything aligned and perfect.

She was no longer able to lie still. Her breath was coming in gasps. Each thrust of Will's body lifted her to another plateau, and she was climbing higher and higher into something fuzzy and beautiful that fogged her mind and dizzied her senses.

And then, suddenly, it was within reach. Whimpers came from her throat. She clasped her lover tighter and urged him deeper into her heat. Release hit her hard, spasms of pleasure that radiated outward from a soft, molten central core.

Her moans and movements told Will the full story. He let himself go and cried out before she had calmed. Then all was quiet. His earlier exhaustion returned tenfold, and he literally collapsed upon her.

It seemed to Clover that it took forever for her to breathe normally. The man in her arms was heavy, but she only smiled. A satisfaction she couldn't have visualized before this made her feel languorous and drowsy.

"Are you falling asleep?" she whispered.

Will raised his head. "Almost. Clover, I wasn't a virgin, but I wish I had been."

She put her forefinger to his lips. "Don't. It's all right." She smiled. "You're a marvel in bed, Will Lang."

He grinned. "You ain't seen nothin' yet, Miss Clover."

"Is that a fact?" she questioned pertly.

Will kissed her and rolled away. "Don't go away. I'll be right back."

"Where would I go?" she asked dreamily as he disappeared into the bathroom. She sighed then, long and lazily, enjoying the serene aftermath of lovemaking. Remembering that she'd whispered words of love during the height of passion, she wondered if Will had heard them.

He came back and stood by the bed. Clover's gaze roamed his nudity with intense admiration. "Would you like me to turn out the lights in the other rooms, honey?" Will asked.

"Please."

The flash of his tight buttocks as he left the bedroom made her smile. Her Will. Her lover. How incredible.

He returned again and climbed into bed. Releasing a long sigh, he snuggled around her. "I'd like to talk now, but I'm so tired I can't think straight."

"That's fine, we can talk in the morning."

"You're an angel, Clover Dove."

"Good night, Will."

"Good night, sweetheart."

Eleven

It amazed and annoyed Clover that she was still awake two hours later. Her eyes, for some reason, would not stay closed. Will was having no such trouble as he'd gone instantly to sleep and hadn't moved a muscle since.

She checked the digital clock a dozen times, lamenting her sleeplessness with the passing minutes. Maybe its cause was nothing more than sharing her bed. She'd slept alone all of her life, and Will took up a lot of space.

That wasn't it, though. She had snuggled down with Will, happy and contented, thrilled that he was with her.

Or so she'd believed.

Then the restlessness had started, the urge to squirm, the determination to fall asleep, the stiffness in her body that wouldn't relent no matter what she did. She tried to meditate, to think of something pleasant and soothing, such as a gently rolling surf or a quiet green meadow.

The meadow and the surf didn't work. Her thoughts turned to her parents, to their volatile, on-again off-again marriage. To the countless times in her memory when they'd both been out of town—not together—and the times they'd both been *in* town and arguing. To the birthdays and holidays they'd missed because of commitments elsewhere.

Clover sighed with what felt like melancholy. Will planned that they would talk in the morning, and she'd have to be incredibly dense to not know which subject was on his agenda. *I love you, Clover. Will you marry me?*

And what was she going to say? She did love him, that was no longer a gray area. And for her, the natural conclusion for two people in love was marriage. But what about birthdays and holidays? Was it petty for a woman to want the man she loved beside her on special occasions?

In all fairness to herself, there was a lot more to her disquietude than birthdays. She wanted children, a real home, a husband who was at the dinner table every night. She loved Will; she probably always would. But did she want to marry him with his present vocation?

Lying there, trying to be still, Clover could hear her own overfast heartbeat. There was no regret in her system for making love with Will, but unease about the future was real enough to raise her blood pressure.

It was a matter of putting him off in the morning, of evading that disturbingly serious discussion. Could she do that without hurting his feelings? Without making him angry? Without saying straight out, "I'll marry you if you quit the music business"?

The thought of putting it so bluntly made Clover queasy. She still couldn't lay down ultimatums. Will had to make his career decision without her influence.

Too on edge to force herself to lie still any longer, Clover slipped out of bed, moving slowly and silently to avoid disturbing Will. She found her robe and put it on in the dark, then tiptoed from the bedroom.

In the living room she snapped on one small lamp. From there she could see the foyer and Will's luggage. There were two suitcases and a guitar case. Balled up and wrinkled on one of the suitcases was what appeared to be a jacket, which Will must have dropped there and she hadn't noticed.

She moved to the foyer automatically, having nothing better to do at such an ungodly hour, and rescued Will's jacket with the intention of hanging it in the foyer closet. She gave it a shake to dislodge some of its wrinkles and started for the closet. An envelope fluttered to the floor, apparently having fallen out of a pocket.

Clover stooped over and picked up the envelope. There was one word on it, "Will," handwritten in pink ink.

The envelope wasn't sealed, and Clover could see that it contained a piece of folded paper. Something intense gripped her vitals. A note? From whom? A woman, obviously. Men didn't use pink ink.

Clover stood there and stared at the envelope while her stomach knotted. She abhorred the feeling of jealousy clutching and clawing at her, but she couldn't get rid of it.

But neither could she remove that piece of paper from the envelope and read whatever was written on it. Locating a pocket in the jacket, she rammed the envelope into it and with jerky, half-frozen movements, opened the closet door and grabbed a hanger.

Will had not come from another woman to her, she told herself fiercely on her way to the kitchen. But this was exactly the sort of incident she could not picture herself living with for the rest of her life. Finding notes, hearing rumors, spending too much time alone and worrying about what Will might be doing in another city. How had her parents' marriage survived at all? They must have very powerful feelings for each other to maintain even their rocky keel.

Clover microwaved a mug of water for tea. When the drink was ready, she brought it to her "messy room" and sat in one of the recliner chairs.

Her thoughts were not comforting. Memory evoked images of Billy and Francine arguing, of herself as a girl watching out a window for one of them to get home. She had never been left alone, but the housekeepers and sitters, however efficient and kind, had not replaced her parents. She had grown up vowing to be there for her own children, and with adulthood, she had also vowed that their father would be there, too.

She was glad that Will had remembered protection tonight. She did not want a pregnancy at this stage in her life.

Her longtime dream of living on a farm, hopefully with a loving husband and babies, felt more unrealistic than ever. Will preferred a house over an apartment, which was admirable, but how often would he be home to enjoy it?

Tears filled Clover's eyes. Love wasn't enough. In fact, falling in love with the wrong man was just possibly the most painful thing a woman could experience.

And she had to let him know how she felt in the morning.

Will opened his eyes and saw nothing familiar. Another hotel room, another...

No! He sat up abruptly. This was Clover's bedroom. Where was she?

Sunlight was filtering through the blinds. The room was pretty and bright with its yellow and white decor. Will glanced at the bed-side clock, which stated in digital numbers that it was seven-thirty.

He threw the sheet back and reached for his jeans. He felt great and grinned while he yanked them on. Going into the bathroom, he rubbed his whiskery jaw and then splashed water on his face. He needed his things for a shower and shave, and his toothbrush. Everything had been left in the foyer.

Leaving Clover's bedroom, he padded barefoot through the living room. The condo was silent. Frowning, he began to look for Clover. His first thought was that she had finished the night in a guest room, although why she would do that eluded him. Turning the knob of a door in the hallway, he peered into an empty bedroom.

She wasn't in the kitchen, either, so he went to her catchall room. That's where she was, sound asleep on a recliner.

Will stood in the doorway and studied her thoughtfully. Questions pestered him, and he suddenly didn't feel so great. Last night was almost vivid enough to touch. Last night had been incredible, and just looking at Clover stirred his blood again.

But why in hell was she sleeping on a chair?

Slowly turning away, Will went to the foyer, took up one of his suitcases and returned to Clover's bathroom. He showered and shaved with a gutful of unpleasant premonitions. Something was wrong, damned wrong. She had belonged to him last night, but she wasn't his this morning. She was a changeable person, he already knew that. And from the events at Bear Creek, she apparently got peculiar revelations during the night.

But he didn't completely buy that "revelations in the night" theory. There was something bothering Clover, something she wasn't talking about. What was it? He didn't doubt that she was as drawn to him as he was to her. Last night proved how deeply her feelings went.

If he hadn't been so beat they would have talked. Maybe she would have told him what was eating at her. This morning he'd bet almost anything that he wouldn't be able to drag it out of her.

He thought of waking her and instead went to the kitchen and found the fixings for a pot of coffee. He was sitting at the table with a cup when she walked in.

Her gaze met his briefly and slid away. "Good morning."

"Morning, honey."

"I'm going to shower. Be back in a few minutes."

"Take your time. I'm not going anywhere."

Clover's jaw was clenched when she hurried away. That discussion was eminent; it was written all over Will's handsome face. And just how was she going to evade it? How?

She stopped at her bedroom door and looked at the bed. Will had straightened the bedding, but the spread was sort of lopsided. Her heart suddenly felt broken. Her eyes misted over. What kind of woman could deliberately drive away the only man she had ever loved?

But then she thought of the envelope with the pink ink, brushed at her tears and went on to the bathroom.

Will was on his third cup of coffee when Clover returned. Her clothing was a blue and white print skirt and a white sleeveless blouse. Her hair was shiny and swingy, and there was makeup on her face. She looked beautiful and the sight of her made his belly ache.

She smiled, but Will saw it as a forced effort. The spasm in his belly got worse.

He tried to speak teasingly. "Do you prefer sleeping in a chair over a bed?"

Clover smoothed her hair and went to a cabinet for a cup. "I was restless and didn't want to disturb you."

"Considerate of you," he commented dryly. He altered his tone. "Sorry I conked out so fast last night."

"I understood. You were exhausted when you got here, and—" She stopped. It was only natural that making love so intensely had added to his exhaustion, but she certainly didn't need to spell it out. She leaned on the counter and sipped her coffee.

"Come and sit down," Will said softly. "I won't bite, I promise."

She colored and changed the subject. "What would you like for breakfast?"

Will looked at her for an awfully long time before replying. "Tell me what's bothering you, Clover."

She took a deep breath. "Denying that something's bothering me would be silly—and futile—I suppose."

"It's pretty obvious, honey. Won't you tell me about it?"

The defense she had devised wasn't distinct in her mind, but it was there, vague and troubling. Not the truth. The truth was too clear, if anything.

"I'm...just not ready for...for what happened last night." Clover eyed him and waited for a response.

He sat there, his expression revealing little of what he might be thinking, and finally said, "You've never taken another man into your bed. That's significant, Clover."

This was one point she could be honest about. "I've never been so attracted to another man."

"And that's all it is between us, attraction? Chemistry?"

Clover's gaze dropped to the cup in her hands. "I'm afraid so."

Will got up slowly. "So how do you see the two of us from now on?"

Her eyes jerked up. "I'm not sure I understand."

"Well, let me put it another way. Is one time together enough, or are you still 'attracted' to me this morning? If you are, I'll be glad to oblige, because once *isn't* enough for me."

Clover felt herself going pale. She hadn't expected bitterness or cynicism from Will, and that's what she was hearing. "I hoped to keep this...friendly," she said unsteadily.

"Friendly enough to go to bed with me again?"

Her knees were shaking. "I didn't expect crudity from you."

"No? What *did* you expect? A smile? A pat on the back? What, Clover? What did you think I'd say when you made your little announcement?"

"I don't know what I thought! But what is anger going to accomplish?" This was not going at all well. How *had* she expected Will to take it?

At least he was keeping his distance. He looked so handsome this morning, and now she didn't have to wonder what was behind his snaps and zipper. She knew it all, how his body looked and felt, what making love with him was like, how tremendously moved one person could be by another.

"All right," Will said stonily. "We'll keep it friendly. But I think you owe me an explanation. We've had a lot to say to each other on the phone. I came here last night—at your request—and you were as loving as anyone could be. Now, this morning, I'm supposed to believe that the whole thing is nothing more than hormones. It's pretty tough to swallow, Clover.''

Clover stirred uneasily. He was not going to let her get by with evasion and vagueness, and she couldn't tell him the truth. What should she do? Shaking in her shoes was getting her nowhere, and besides, maybe there was a small pocket of indignation in the back of her mind. After all, she wasn't the one receiving notes written with sizzling pink ink!

She squared her shoulders and leveled a close to frosty gaze on him. ''You've slept with other women. Do you expect me to believe that every occasion was more than hormones?''

Will looked slightly shell-shocked. ''What I did before I knew you has nothing to do with now. If it were possible for me to undo my past relationships, I'd do it in a heartbeat. And just so you know, there weren't that many.''

Clover looked away. ''All I'm asking is that you accept my decision to remain uninvolved.'' She looked at him again. ''I don't think that's an unreasonable request.''

''But we *are* involved!''

''We're on the *edge* of involvement! I just don't plan to go over!''

''All right, fine! Tell me what happens the next time you're *attracted* to someone! Will you take him to bed, too?''

Clover's mouth dropped open. ''How dare you! You of all people should be a better judge of my character. If you're deliberately trying to infuriate me, you're succeeding!''

Will ran agitated fingers through his hair. ''I'm not trying to do anything but get at the truth. Clover, you're keeping something from me. I don't know what it is and I'm beginning to wonder if even you know. Maybe it's something you haven't faced, some feeling or instinct that you haven't recognized."

"Don't be absurd."

"What's absurd about it? I'm going in circles and you're not making it any easier." Broodingly Will stared at her with his hands on his hips. "What do you want me to do, walk out of here and pretend last night never happened?"

She avoided looking at his eyes. "I don't think pretense is necessary. I hope we can still be friends."

Will was silent for a painfully long stretch. "I don't understand you."

"I'm sorry."

"Are you? Somehow I don't get that impression."

"I'm sorry about that, too."

"Why did you go to bed with me last night?" Will questioned bluntly.

Her eyes moved to his. "I told you."

"What you told me is a crock!" he shouted, and immediately closed his eyes and took several deep breaths. "You're tying me in knots. Why do you want me to believe that attraction got the better of you? And if you were so damned *attracted* that you couldn't control it, why don't you give it more importance?"

"What do you want me to say, Will, that I fell in love with you?"

His eyes narrowed. "Yeah, maybe that's exactly what I want you to say."

"If I had, would we be having this discussion?" She was on the verge of caving in. If he didn't accept her verdict and leave soon, she was apt to renege on every vow and throw herself into his arms.

How masculine he was, how handsome. Tall and valiant and wearing a hurt expression because he didn't understand. She could clear up his perplexity with a few words. *I can't love you because you'll only bring me heartache. I want normal. I want ordinary. You're not an ordinary man. I thought you were, but you're not.*

"We're arguing and there's nothing to argue about," Will said grimly. "You want me, you don't want me. You're like the bouncing ball in those old musical movie shorts." He shaped a cynical smile. "Do you think you'll want me again one of these days? Should I call and find out, or wait until you get the urge and call me?"

Clover slammed her coffee cup down on the counter. "That's enough! I don't owe you anything, Will Lang. You enjoyed what happened last night, and if I don't want further involvement, I don't have to have it!"

"Yeah, I enjoyed it. But so did you."

"Did I say I didn't? Didn't I admit more attraction to you than any man I've ever known? Attraction doesn't automatically indicate permanency, you know. With your background, you must know that a heck of a lot better than I do!"

"You don't know anything about my background, so don't bring it into the conversation."

Clover threw up her hands. "You're right! Forget I said anything about it."

Will's eyes narrowed again. "Are you upset because I wasn't a virgin?"

"Good Lord, no! I didn't expect you to be. It never once occurred to me you might not have been with a string of women."

"There wasn't a *string,* dammit! Clover, this is getting ridiculous. What do you want me to do? Are you and I through?" Will's expression softened. "Honey, you mean an awful lot to me. Please tell me what's really bothering you."

"Your ego is astounding. You simply cannot accept the fact that once was enough for me, can you?"

Will's eyes picked up a dangerous glitter. "That's it in a nutshell, I guess." He took three long strides and grabbed her around the waist with his left arm, hauling her to him while clasping the back of her head with his right hand.

Unprepared for so much physicality, she teetered against him with shock on her face. His mouth descended and captured hers. Her mind reeled and she pushed against his chest, but he was too solidly planted to move.

She became breathless very quickly. Thrills compounded in her body until she couldn't think, and still the kiss went on. His tongue demanded entrance to her mouth. His fingers kneaded her scalp. His body rubbed against hers in the most wanton way possible, and in the dim recesses of her brain she realized how hard and aroused he was.

And she wasn't offended. Neither was she angry. The love she felt for Will Lang was surfacing with alarming speed. A low moan built in her throat. Her heart was beating wildly. He was big and overwhelming and bringing last night back in sweltering waves.

But he was different this morning, not so patient, not so giving. Rough. Almost primitive.

She liked him this way. She loved the feeling of his hard body against hers, the sensation of being overpowered by his passion, the rising heat in her own system. Last night had been perfect, but she'd had nothing to compare it with. This sort of unleashed emotion was completely foreign to her, but nothing in her life had ever been so exciting.

Her body grew tenser and writhed with his. Her hands began roaming. Her mouth opened and challenged his.

At her unexpected response, a rush of adrenaline nearly staggered Will. He cupped her face and lavished kisses on her lips, her chin, her cheeks, whispering, "Baby...oh, Baby." She was alluring, inviting, the embodiment of womankind, everything and anything a man could hope for in a mate.

Her back was to the counter. His hands moved down, caressing her throat, then her breasts. Their kisses became frenetic, gasping. He lifted her, settling her on the counter, and her legs went around him.

The buttons on her blouse gave easily. He pushed it from her shoulders while she did the same with his shirt. Dazed from the hunger storming her, Clover groped as recklessly as Will. She adored his chest with its pattern of black hair and hard muscles, and the way his belly rippled. His manhood was straining the seams, and she unzipped his fly and freed him.

Her panties were drawn down; she would never know how. But one second the flimsy garment was in place and the next it wasn't. His mouth covered hers, and in the next pulse beat he was in her.

The room spun. Her eyes closed while she moaned at the lust she felt. The wealth of wanting. The need, oh, the need of him.

His thrusts were not gentle. Rather, there was a savagery in their coupling that had been totally absent last night. Her very skin demanded and responded, air was taken in short pants.

"Look at me," he growled.

Her gaze locked with his. She dampened her parted lips. Everything was sensation, from the perspiration on her temples to the joyous pleasure in her body. His height made their positions perfect for making love, but never in a million years could she have imagined such behavior on her kitchen counter.

And it wasn't at all the way last night had been. There was precious little gentleness on Will's face, let alone in his commanding rhythm. Unquestionably he was in control and intended to remain so.

Her own intentions were murky, unimportant in the face of so much raw emotion. She rested her forearms on his shoulders and looked into his eyes, with her face flushed and moist and her body eager for anything he might do.

Her skirt was bunched between them. She couldn't see what was happening, she could only feel it. His powerful thrusts, her own reactions. On and on. Again and again. Her chest kept getting tighter and tighter. He dipped his head and pressed his mouth to hers, and his tongue took up the same tempo as his body.

Her breaths became shorter, more labored. She could hear the harsh heaviness of his breathing. And then she couldn't breathe at all and tore her mouth free, turning her head and laying it on his shoulder.

The pressure in her lower body was becoming unbearable. "Don't stop," she moaned. "Don't stop."

"Baby, I couldn't stop if I wanted to," Will mumbled thickly.

The incredible pleasure she remembered from last night began. It was the same but more intense, piercingly intense. She clutched his head and cried out in a series of guttural sounds. Her thighs tightened around him. "Yes...oh, yes!"

Will's release was only seconds beyond hers. "Clover...*Baby!*"

She started trembling. The counter was almost instantly uncomfortable. She leaned into Will and felt him shaking, as well.   He raised his head and looked at her. "Guess the attraction is still there."

Her tongue circled her lips, moistening them. "Guess it is."

His eyes were no longer glittering. In fact, Clover saw only somberness in their dark blue depths. "It's always going to be there, Baby."

She swallowed. How could she deny anything he might say at this point?

Will saw her confusion. "Don't worry. I'm not going to pressure you into a commitment."

Clover's eyes widened. "You're not?"

"Nope." Will laid a tender kiss on her forehead, moved away from her and turned his back.

It struck Clover then that he hadn't used protection. Biting her lower lip, she slid from the counter, scooped up her panties from the floor and fled from the kitchen.

When she returned ten minutes later, Will was sitting on one of his suitcases in the foyer. He stood up. "Do you want me to call you or not?"

Hot color flooded Clover's face. Had he merely used her in the kitchen? It had been so incredible for her. Hadn't it been as good for him? She was wavering on her previous stand, she knew. How could she insist they be only friends with so much passion between them?

But he seemed only resigned to her former attitude. Pride lifted her chin, when she really felt like weeping.

"Call if you want," she said evenly. This was unbelievable. How could they be standing here as though nothing had happened? They'd just made love on her kitchen counter, the *counter,* for God's sake!

He hesitated then nodded. "All right. Be talking to you one of these days."

Stunned, Clover watched him pick up his suitcases, juggling them so he could also carry his guitar case. "But... but you don't have a car."

"I called a taxi. It should be here any minute. Mind opening the door for me?"

Oh, my God. Clover's legs nearly gave out, but she managed to open the door without revealing her numbing shock.

Will had just stepped out onto the stoop when the taxi pulled up to the curb. He turned around to face Clover. "Well, what do I say now?"

"I don't know." *Please, please don't say something hurting... or funny... or teasing.*

He regarded her for a long moment, then smiled faintly. "How about if I just say I love you? Think that constitutes a friendly goodbye?" He bent forward and kissed her lips. "So long, Baby. I'll be in touch."

Clover stood there, as stiff as a statue, while he walked to the taxi and got in. It wasn't until the cab was out of sight that she finally turned and went back into the condo.

Twelve

Clover wasn't entirely clear on what had happened with Will that morning. Their lovemaking was a decidedly arousing memory but still perturbing. Their argument hadn't gone anywhere, and in retrospect seemed to be so much dust in a high wind. Obviously she'd hurt Will, which hadn't been her intention, and she felt terrible about it. But how could she have explained herself? An explanation in this case would merely be an ultimatum in disguise.

The only relatively distinct thing about the whole episode was Will telling her that he loved her, and deep down Clover wasn't completely positive she'd heard that right. Take intonation, for instance. How had he really sounded? Had he spoken sarcastically? Cynically? Maybe teasingly. What had he really hoped to convey with that tantalizing departure?

She moped around the condo hoping Will would call. Something stopped her from calling him—pride, maybe, although there wasn't any question about her still disliking Will's present career. It just seemed so awful, all of it. She loved him, he perhaps loved her and they were both being stubborn. Or, at least, she was.

It was several days later that she went to the foyer closet for two dresses that she'd hung in there, which needed to go to the cleaners. The sight of Will's jacket stopped her. He'd gone off without it and she certainly hadn't been thinking about jackets that morning.

She stared for a moment, then slipped her hand into the side pocket. The envelope was still there. She jerked her hand back quickly. The damned thing! She still couldn't read whatever was written on that piece of paper, but unquestionably that pink ink had wreaked a little havoc with her nervous system the other morning.

Clover heaved a long-suffering sigh. That envelope was just so reminiscent of some of the trials and tribulations that Billy and Francine were forced to face periodically. Notes, rumors, extended separations, fame, too much adulation and acclamation—that was the music business for you.

Another day passed. Realizing that she had to get on with her life, Clover called John Domaney to ask if he was working on any records or videos for which she might sing backup. He told her to check back in a week or so. With that avenue of activity on hold, she threw herself into her charities.

One evening Billy and Francine dropped in. Francine was resplendent in a black-and-fuchsia pantsuit and matching boots, and Billy was in one of his usual costumes of worn jeans, big hat and snakeskin boots.

Genuinely glad to see her parents, Clover hugged then invited them to have a seat in the living room. She was dying to ask about Will, but didn't want to be the first to bring up his name. She didn't have to wait long.

"When we told Will we were coming over here, he said to say hello," Francine volunteered brightly.

Clover adopted a nonchalant expression. "How is he?"

"Fine, fine," Billy replied, almost gravely.

"He's still staying with you?" Clover questioned. Both Billy and Francine nodded. "I thought he only planned to stay at your house for a few days."

"Oh, there's no hurry," Francine said. "We kind of like having him around, don't we, honey?"

Billy confirmed his wife's comment. "Sure do. We like Will a heap, Baby."

"That's nice." Actually Clover felt as if she'd just eaten some sour grapes. Her mouth was pursed and she knew it. Deliberately she changed the subject. "So, when's your next tour, Mother?"

"Not for another two months. Billy's got one coming up, though."

Clover's heart sank. "When?"

Billy smiled serenely. "In about two weeks. Came up sort of sudden like. Didn't really expect it."

Clover stood up. "Let me get you something to drink. Is coffee all right?"

"Coffee's fine," said both parents.

Nearly running to the kitchen, Clover gritted her teeth. Will would be gone again in two lousy weeks. For how long?

She hurried back to the living room doorway. "How long will your tour last, Billy?"

He smiled again. "Oh, it's a good one, Baby. The whole West Coast. We'll be gone for over a month."

"Wonderful." Again that sour taste was in her mouth. Steeling herself, Clover returned to the kitchen and prepared the coffeepot.

This whole thing had gone far enough. Did she love Will Lang?

Yes!

Did he love her?

He said so, didn't he? What do you want, eggs in your beer? How much plainer do you need?

Clover Dove was not ordinarily a hand-wringer, but when the coffeepot was switched on and beginning to gurgle, she caught herself holding her own hands and worrying them.

Forcing her jumpy hands to her sides, she went back to the living room and sat down. "The coffee will be ready in a few minutes."

Francine smiled. "Wonderful."

Billy smiled. "What a fine little hostess you are."

Clover's gaze darted from parent to parent. There was something funny going on. If that wasn't a cat-eating-the-canary expression on those two faces, she'd never seen one. Now that she thought about it, when was the last time Billy and Francine—at the same time, yet—had casually dropped in?

"Frannie," Billy said. "Remember when I told you about that superdelicious fruit salad Clover made at Will's house?"

"I remember," Francine said.

"And her corn bread melted in my mouth. Will was impressed, I don't mind telling you."

Clover had heard enough. "Just what is going on with you two?" she questioned bluntly. Billy and Francine both arranged innocent expressions that only made Clover more leery. "Something is, so don't think you're pulling the wool over my eyes."

"Good heavens, you're suspicious," Francine declared.

"You bet your sweet bippy, I am," Clover retorted. "Did Will send you over here?"

"Clover," Billy said solemnly. "Your mother and I would never interfere in your private life."

Oh, yeah? Since when? Clover clamped her lips together before her skepticism escaped. What was wrong with her parents was their glee. Yes, that was it. Underneath those purposely innocent expressions was glee, and lots of it. They were practically bursting, in fact.

She sat back. "Will and I aren't seeing each other anymore. Did he tell you?"

Francine and Billy exchanged glances. "Didn't know a thing about it," Billy said evenly. "Too bad, honey. We like Will a heap."

So you said. "Well . . . it's over between us," Clover announced flatly. "Never was anything important, anyway." She almost laughed at the startled look on Billy's face, and a glance at Francine resulted in the same reaction.

"Now don't be hasty, Baby," Billy cautioned.

"But I thought . . ." Francine stammered. "Clover, you said you liked Will."

"I do like him. Am I supposed to marry every man I like?"

Billy cleared his throat. "Frannie, I just remembered a phone call I have to make. We have to go home."

"You may use my phone," Clover offered with a sweet smile.

"No . . . no, thanks." Billy got to his feet. "Come on, honey, let's go home."

When her parents had gone, Clover went to the kitchen and turned off the coffeepot. She stood there for a moment, wondering what in heck the past few minutes had been all about. Billy and Francine knew something that she didn't, but what? Obviously it had to do with Will. Such smugness when they'd arrived, such confusion when they'd left! Oh, yes, they knew something, and it was something they had never intended telling her. So, what had they come for, to test her pulse on Will? What on earth had he told them?

Clover went to bed that night thinking about it. Maybe she should call Will. Whatever he'd told the excitable Doves, it hadn't been that he and Clover weren't seeing each other. That information had nearly knocked Billy's and Francine's expensive boots off their feet.

Maybe she would call Will if he weren't leaving Nashville again in two weeks.

Turning over, Clover punched her pillow. Nothing had changed, not one blasted thing. She loved a music man, dammit, a *music man!*

Four days later—Clover was counting—Will called. "Hi, Baby. This is Will."

"Hello, Will." Clover's heart had nearly stopped at the sound of his voice, but her response was as cool as if he were a stranger.

"What'cha doing on this beautiful Saturday morning?"

"Nothing much. A little house cleaning, this and that."

"Care to take a ride?"

Clover clutched the phone tighter. "A ride where?"

"Oh, just out into the country."

A ride in the country. Why? After telling her he loved her, he'd stayed completely away. There hadn't even been a phone call for over a week.

"Well...I don't know," she said slowly. Actually her pulse was misbehaving something awful. She could not turn her affection for Will Lang off and on like a light bulb. Not anymore she couldn't. Didn't she go to sleep every night thinking about making love with him? Didn't she see his smile in her mind's eye almost constantly?

Life was a torment these days. Nothing was fun, food was tasteless, friends were boring. She was focused on Will, and nothing else had much meaning.

"Is it a major decision?" Will teased. "There's a lot of sunshine out there just going to waste, Baby."

Clover glanced out the nearest window. A day with Will. A day in the sun, riding around in the country with Will.

"You're right," she conceded. "I can be ready in half an hour."

"I'll be there. See you soon."

Will was friendly but distant. Physically distant, that is. He didn't try to kiss or touch her when he picked her up and opened the passenger door of his car for her to get in.

But Clover was thinking of kissing and touching. She couldn't look at Will without thinking of kissing and touching. While he drove, she cast furtive glances his way, studying him in quick spurts, his profile, his snowy-white Western shirt, the fit of his jeans.

The fit of his jeans was particularly fascinating. He had marvelous thighs, long and sinewy and filling the worn denim to perfection. And his fly...damn. Was she becoming one of those women who couldn't keep her eyes off of a man's fly?

Will was all smiles and charm this morning, acting, Clover thought warily, as though they'd parted a week ago on the best of terms. As though they hadn't argued and then made frantic love on her kitchen counter.

She sighed and faced front, registering then that Will had taken Cummings Road. Clover approved of Will's direction. Cummings Road led to some of the prettiest farming country in the area.

For the next twenty minutes, their conversation consisted of admiring remarks about the scenery. "Oh, that place is lovely," was Clover's observation about a sprawling farm with every building painted an eye-catching, smoky blue-gray.

"Take a look at that field," Will commented while passing a brilliant green pasture with white fencing.

There were truck farms with fields of vegetables, and farms with cotton crops. Some were truly spectacular. Clover enjoyed seeing them all, both large and small, affluent and modest.

Will made a left turn and then after a few miles, a right turn, and Clover began seeing country she'd never been in before. Again the conversation was about the scenery. There were more trees, the road followed a series of rolling hills, but there were still farms tucked into hollows and between forests.

It was pretty country, beautiful to the eye and peaceful to the senses. Clover found herself fully relaxed and enjoying the ride. She looked at Will and smiled.

"What?" he questioned, sensing her scrutiny.

"I was just thinking."

"About what?"

"That I'm enjoying this. Thanks for asking me to come with you."

"Thought you might like it."

"Mind if I roll down the window?"

"Help yourself," Will replied.

Clover pushed the window button on the armrest and breathed in the fresh air that instantly ruffled her hair. "I love it out here," she murmured. "Someday I'm going to live on a farm, I swear it."

Will laughed softly. "All by yourself?"

"If necessary."

"What would you plant?"

Clover shrugged. "I have no idea. Depends on the type of soil one has, doesn't it?"

"I'm as green about farms as you are, but that makes sense."

"Maybe I'll raise horses," Clover mused as they passed a field with about thirty graceful roan horses.

"I like that idea."

Clover nodded. "So do I. Of course, I don't know much about horses, either. Anyone can learn, though."

"Sure can, honey."

That was the first familiarity out of Will's mouth, and Clover sent him a curious sidelong glance. The strongest urge to open up with him was suddenly overwhelming. *Will, quit the band. I love you and I think you love me, too. We could live on a farm. We could raise horses and kids and...*

She couldn't say it, she just couldn't.

Will stopped the car at the side of the road. Clover saw a cut in the trees and something else, a For Sale sign on a rather dilapidated barbed-wire fence. She looked at Will questioningly.

"Want to take a look?" he asked. At her hesitation, he added, "Let's do it. What do you say?"

"You'd like to see it?"

"I would. Just for the fun of it."

"Well . . . all right. It might be fun."

Will pulled onto the dirt road in the trees, which very quickly proved to be a driveway. The trees opened up onto a large clearing. There was a big old house and about a half-dozen outbuildings of various sizes. Some rusted machinery adorned the area. Fences sagged as well as the house's front porch.

There was no one around and the place appeared to have been vacant for a long time. Will braked and turned off the engine. A lovely silence drifted through the car's open window. Clover peered at the house, which was two stories of fading siding and peeling paint.

But there was a splendid porch that stretched all along the front of the house and down one side. There were brick chimneys. There were several trellises with neglected, partially dried-out rosebushes. And there was a swing on the porch.

"Do we dare peek in the windows?" Clover asked.

Will looked at her. "I doubt that the owner would mind. Do you like it?"

Clover opened her door. "It's got a great deal of potential." She climbed out of the car and waited for Will to join her.

They trudged across the dying lawn to the porch stairs. Clover went immediately to some tall, narrow windows and cupped her eyes to see in. "Oh, my," she said softly.

"What?"

"It's got hardwood floors, and I can see a fireplace with a marble mantel."

Will began snooping around. "I'll bet there's a key somewhere out here."

Clover turned. "We shouldn't, Will."

He bent down and turned back a crusty old mat lying near the door. "Here it is." With a key in his hand, he straightened up. "Want to see inside?"

Clover cast a worried glance at the driveway. "What if someone comes along?"

Will fit the key into the front door lock and turned it. "Come on, worrywart. Let's explore."

She couldn't resist and followed Will into the house. Once inside, she went from room to room ahead of Will. "Look at the woodwork!"

"Needs refinishing."

"And these floors. Will, you don't see this kind of flooring in new houses."

"It's all scarred and scuffed."

"The kitchen has iron sinks! This place must be a hundred years old!"

"Sixty-five."

Clover stopped and looked at him. "Sixty-five? How do you know?"

Will took her by the hand. "Come and see the back of the place."

Frowning, Clover let herself be led along. "You've been here before, haven't you?"

He opened a door and positioned her to see through it to the outside, standing directly behind her with his hands on her shoulders. "There are two hundred acres. See that fence way off to the left?"

"I see it."

"That's one boundary line. Now look to the right. Bypass the first fence and look way out to the second. That's the right boundary line. It goes straight back to that big stand of trees."

Clover tried to turn around, but Will said softly, "Please don't. Just stand here like we're doing and absorb the beauty of this place."

It was difficult to stand still when her heart was pounding and a dozen questions burned her brain. He'd been here before. Why had he brought her back to see it? Why was he standing so close? What was he thinking?

After a minute the questions subsided. Will was behind her, tall and warm, with his big hands on her upper arms, and his nearness was the best thing she'd felt since that final, fateful morning.

He spoke very quietly. "I've something to say. Will you hear me out?"

"I'll listen," she said in a husky, low voice.

"I love you, Clover. I want you to marry me. After the last time we were together, I know I'm taking a hell of a chance. But I put a conditional deposit on this place. The condition is your approval. Not a partial approval, a one-hundred percent approval. It was once a thriving farm and it can be again. We could grow anything we wanted to out here, or raise horses." A little squeak came out of Clover's throat. "What did you say?" Will asked.

She tried again and only made another weird sound.

"I know it needs a lot of work," Will hastened to say. "But I'm good with a hammer and saw. There are newer places for sale if you don't like this one, but when I saw it, it just reached right out and grabbed me."

Clover was getting so choked up she was afraid of doing something ridiculous, like bursting into tears. This was her dream, her fantasy. The place grabbed her, too. All too easily she could see herself and Will living here, working together to remodel, paint, repair and filling it with furniture.

But there was another image interfering with the best part of that vision: Will leaving her out here alone while he traveled with Billy's band.

Dear God, what was she going to do? The man behind her was the only one she would ever love. He made her come alive; he was sweet and kind and perfect in every way.

She swallowed the lump of tears in her throat. "I...I like the place," she whispered.

"And me?" Will slowly turned her around and looked into her eyes. "Do you like me, too?"

Clover knew that she'd lost the battle, but maybe that was okay when the war was finally over. "I more than like you, Will. I love you."

Excitement suddenly gleamed in Will's eyes. "And you'll marry me?"

"I'll marry you."

He whooped and grabbed her into a bear hug, lifting her clean off the floor. Clover laughed because his elation was contagious.

He settled down and held her close to his chest. She could hear his strong, fast heartbeat. "Oh, Baby, life is sure good."

She closed her eyes. "Yes...life is good."

He began kissing her, her eyelids, her cheeks, her lips. "I love you so much," he whispered. "Clover, I've never been in love with another woman. I want you to know that."

"I've never been in love before, either."

"You're an incredible woman."

She knew that he was referring to her virginity. "You're very sweet, Will."

He raised his head and regarded her soberly. "Are you sure about this place?"

"I think it's wonderful."

"I'll make it perfect for you. It'll be like new when I'm done, I promise."

Clover smiled. "*We'll* make it perfect."

His eyes were getting smoky, she saw, and her breath caught because she knew what was in his mind. He held her face and kissed her mouth, a slow, sensual mating of lips and tongues that weakened her knees. It was all right. She would make love with Will wherever and whenever the mood struck.

And she wanted him, oh, how she wanted him. She smiled inwardly, knowing now why she had put on a dress instead of slacks for a ride in the country. And why she wasn't wearing a bra or underpants.

She forgot her own clothing, or lack thereof, and concentrated on Will's. "I love these shirts you wear," she said seductively, and opened his snaps with one fluid flick of her wrist. The fine art of "wrist flicking" had more purposes than just fly-fishing!

Will worked her skirt up and then stared into her eyes. "Why, Miss Clover!"

She laughed deep in her throat. "Surprised you, huh?"

Will laughed, too, but not for long. He was suddenly engrossed in the satin smoothness of her bare behind, which he was caressing as though he'd never touched a nude bottom before.

He kissed her then, groaning hungrily, and his hands never stopped searching. Unable to see what she was doing, Clover managed on instinct and imagination, and she found his fly and opened his zipper.

She took him out of his jeans and felt her fever mounting. "It's...you're fantastic," she whispered against his lips.

"*You're* what's fantastic," he said raggedly. "Baby, we're going to do this a lot, so maybe we shouldn't be so impatient. This place isn't very clean, and there's nothing to lie on."

"Can you really wait until we get back to town?" she whispered, and slid kisses down his chest to the maleness she held in her hands.

He emitted a growl of utter agony at her boldness. "You call it," he said thickly. "I'll do whatever you want."

She eyed the counter, but it was much lower than the one in her condo. The hardwood floors were dusty and there wasn't any furniture at all.

Except for...

Clover grabbed Will's hand and dragged him away from the door. In one room she'd seen an old straight-back chair. She brought Will to it. "Sit."

He grinned and did as she requested. Their eyes met while she straddled his legs, and then he wasn't grinning any longer. He wet his lips with his tongue and held her hips. "Easy," he cautioned hoarsely while she sat down slowly.

She wrapped her arms around his neck. "Oh, Will, there's nothing else like this, nothing."

He held her and moved his hips just a little. He was fully in her, and she was tight and hot and moist. "Raise up," he whispered. "Then come down."

She got the hang of it very quickly. "You're a good teacher."

"You're a good pupil."

They looked at each other while they moved. "I love you," she whispered.

"I love you. For ever and ever, Clover. Nothing will ever separate us, nothing."

"Nothing, my love," she ardently vowed, pushing traitorous thoughts of bands and tours to the back of her mind.

They were getting sweaty. And very excited. Very agitated. They moved faster. The chair emitted a squeak of protest every time Clover came down. She angled her head and opened her mouth on his, kissing him with all of the passion in her heart and soul. All of the love.

It came upon her gradually, gathering in a strange distant place in her body, the same joy she had experienced twice before in Will's arms. And then it was sweeping her along, making her cry out in a way that was still new enough to be unfamiliar to her ears.

But, oh, it was lovely. Delicious. Liquid fire, and wave upon wave of intense pleasure. This time, the first time for her, she fully recognized Will's release. She felt the trembling of his arms and body, heard the unsteady quavering of his voice.

She loved him with every fiber of her being, feeling at once loverlike and maternal toward him. She would see to his needs for the rest of her life, cook his food, bear his children, share his burdens and his joys.

And wait for him to come home when he was gone.

She stroked his hair, the back of his neck, and whispered, "How I love you." She smiled at him. "And this."

"It was perfect. *You're* perfect."

Was that a tear in his eye? Clover tenderly touched his face.

He cleared his throat and shaped a smile. "When can we be married?"

"Soon."

"Do you want a big wedding?"

"Do you honestly think we could get by with something small and quiet with Francine and Billy for parents?"

They looked at each other then threw their heads back and laughed. Billy and Francine Dove would do their best to throw the biggest, splashiest wedding that Nashville had ever seen, and Clover and Will both knew it.

It didn't matter. Everything was wonderful.

Thirteen

———

On the drive back to the city Will said, "You're positive about buying the farm?"

Clover was sitting next to him, using the center seat belt, her left hand riding on his right thigh. They'd spent hours walking the land and examining the house and buildings. "I love it, Will. I'm very positive."

"It's going to be great, honey. I can hardly wait to get started on fixing it up." He hesitated, then said quietly, "Clover, can you tell me now what's been bothering you? I was sure you had feelings for me, but bringing you out here today was taking a very big chance."

"I'm glad you took it." Could she explain herself now? Clover bit her lip. Wouldn't detailing her dislike of the music business only cause hurt feelings? She was accepting Will's career. Wasn't that enough?

"Will, I guess I just didn't know my own mind," she finally said, adding after a moment, "Everything's very clear now."

Will frowned slightly. "That's all it was?"

"That's all." She hugged his arm. "Would you like to know the exact moment that I fell in love with you?"

"Do you know the exact moment?"

"Yes, I do. It was when you opened the door that night in the rain. The night I came to your house to find Billy. You stood there, wearing only a pair of worn jeans, and I nearly fell off of the porch."

Will laughed softly, caught her hand, brought it to his lips and kissed it. "Incredible."

A wonderful contentment filled Clover. "Yes, it was. It is."

"Speaking of Billy, honey, there's something I should tell you."

She snuggled closer. "You can tell me anything."

Will took a deep breath. He'd been dreading this moment, not at all certain of how Clover would feel about it. "I quit the band. I sure do hope you don't mind."

Nearly struck dumb, Clover sat up. "You quit?"

"Professional entertaining's just not for me, Clover. Please understand."

She didn't know if she was going to laugh, cry or fall into a dead faint. He quit the band. *He quit!* And he'd announced it as casually as if he'd been describing the sunny day. No, wait. In his voice there'd been doubt that she would understand.

This was unbelievable. "You've told Billy?"

Will nodded. "Last Tuesday."

"Tuesday?" Wasn't that the evening Francine and Billy had come to the condo? So that's what had been bursting their seams. They'd known that Will was out of the business, and not only hadn't they been unhappy about it, but they'd been glad for her sake.

"Did Billy find a replacement?" she asked softly, unsteadily.

Will nodded, his expression still a little grim. So far Clover hadn't said aye or nay. Was it okay with her, or wasn't it? "Yeah, he did. Did you ever meet Sara Green, by any chance?"

"Sara Green?" Clover echoed in a very small voice. "Is she a guitarist?"

"She's a singer, and a darned good one. But her boyfriend plays real well, and—"

"Her boyfriend! I didn't know she had a boyfriend."

Will cast her an odd glance. "Why wouldn't she have a boyfriend?"

"Uh . . . she would, of course. She's very attractive."

"Anyway, Jake—that's her boyfriend, Jake Lohman— is one heck of a good player. He's taking my place."

Clover was practically speechless. It was too much to absorb at one time. Will was out, *out*, of the business. They were going to be married and living on a farm. Sara Green had her own boyfriend and probably never had been after Billy.

Will felt how stiffly she was sitting. "Are you okay? Honey, I don't want to disappoint you in any way, but I just can't stay in music. I hated that tour, and guess what else was happening. My name was mentioned in an article written about Billy's band. Clover, if I stayed with it, it wouldn't be long before my soul wouldn't be my own."

He felt as if he was pleading for his life. If she hated his decision, things wouldn't be nearly as perfect as he wanted.

Tears began spilling from Clover's eyes. "Oh, Will, you have no idea . . ." She turned her face to his shoulder and started crying into his shirtsleeve.

"My God," Will mumbled, and pulled the car over to the side of the road. He unsnapped his seat belt and hers, then put his arms around her. "Clover, Baby, if you don't want me to quit...honey what's wrong? Tell me why you're crying."

Her sobs garbled her words. "You quit...you don't know...I can't tell you...oh, Will!"

"You can tell me. *Please* tell me." Will tried to lift her chin. "Clover, you *have* to tell me. Here, take my handkerchief."

She accepted the handkerchief and wiped her eyes. Will was staring, and she could tell from his distressed expression that she was worrying him. "Everything's so perfect," she wailed and stuck her face in his shirt again.

He stroked her hair, with his heart beating a mile a minute. "Honey, you're not making any sense."

"I know I'm not." She raised her head and wiped her eyes again. Then she looked directly into his. "Will, I hated your joining Billy's band."

He stared for the longest time and finally mumbled, "You what?"

"I hated it. That's why I kept backing off."

"You're kidding." Will was so stunned he felt numb. "Why didn't you tell me?"

"I couldn't. Think about it. What if you had loved doing it? Wouldn't how I felt about it have torn you apart?" Clover looked down at the damp handkerchief in her hands. "I kept falling deeper in love with you. I tried not to. I didn't want my husband traveling all over the globe. I wanted him home with me."

Elation began building in Will, and he tipped her chin. "Look at me, honey. I'll always be home with you."

Clover's eyes got misty again. "And you made that decision all by yourself. You see? I did the right thing."

"Yes, but you didn't know it until a few minutes ago. Clover, you said you'd marry me before I told you about quitting the band."

Her lower lip trembled. "I couldn't fight my feelings for you any longer. I decided that whatever you wanted to do, if it made you happy, then I would live with it." Her fingertips rose to caress his cheek. "I'm so happy about your decision I could cry."

Intense relief made Will's chuckle a little shaky. "I think that's what you've been doing." He brought her head to his chest and cuddled her. "You know, if you'd told me how you felt, I would have quit immediately."

"No, it had to be your decision." Clover lifted her head to see him. "Francine or Billy never said anything to you about how I felt?"

"They knew?"

"Mother and I talked about it, and yes, Billy had to know, too. I've never made any secret of it, Will." Clover smiled a little sheepishly. "I mentioned wanting a nice, normal, anonymous man several times that I can remember. They had to know."

Will became very still. "Clover, there's nothing wrong with Billy and Francine's way of life. They've made their marriage work for a lot of years, and against some pretty tough odds."

"I agree," she said quietly. "I love and admire them both, Will, enormously. But is it wrong for me to want something different?"

"No, it's not wrong. Different strokes for different folks, honey." Will smiled tenderly. "You and I are alike. Billy and Francine are alike. They're good people, we're good people."

"And we're going to live on a farm." Excitement was replacing the tears in Clover's eyes. "I can't believe it."

"Believe it...and kiss me," Will whispered, and dipped his head to unite their mouths. The kiss started out gentle and unassuming, but quickly evolved into passion. Will gathered her up, pressing her as close to him as was possible. "You're beautiful and so sexy I can't see straight." He looked into her eyes. "If we weren't on a main highway, this would get very hot, very fast."

Grinning crookedly, he got back behind the wheel. Clover formed a glowing smile and snuggled against him. They snapped their seat belts in place and Will started the car moving.

Sitting so close to Will excited Clover. She stood it as long as she could, but about a mile from her condo she undid one snap on Will's shirt and slid her hand inside. "I'm obsessed with you, Will Lang. Obsessed with your body," she whispered into his ear, then took his lobe between her lips and wet it with her tongue.

"When we get to your condo I'll show you who's obsessed," Will mumbled thickly.

"Do you promise?" she whispered seductively. The hand in his shirt drifted downward. "Your belt is awfully tight."

"You can undo it...later."

"Not now?"

"It's broad daylight."

"Do you care?"

Will groaned. "I can't drive with you fooling around."

"We're almost home."

"Thank God."

Smiling, Clover closed her eyes and played with the hair on his chest. There was another area of his body where she intended to do a lot of playing, the thought of which created a roar in her brain. Being in love was wonderful, and there weren't words to accurately describe making love.

Was it like this for everyone in love? Did other people feel the same dreamy, mushy, giddy sensations she did? The same urge to touch and be touched?

Clover opened her eyes when the car came to a stop. "We're home?"

"We're home," Will confirmed, and undid his seat belt. Turning, he clasped her into a fierce embrace. "Now, just what is it that's been going through your mind for the past few minutes?"

"I'll give you three guesses," she purred, and moaned softly when his hand slid under her skirt.

"Thinking of you sitting next to me with nothing under this skirt's been making me crazy," Will whispered. "It's a wonder I didn't drive into a culvert."

She parted her thighs and brought his head down for a kiss. His tongue thrust into her mouth, and when he broke the kiss, his face was flushed. "We'd better go in before I scandalize the neighbors."

"I hate to move," she whispered. "I love your touching me like this."

He slid one finger inside of her. "Like this?"

"Oh, yes." Her face was flushed, too. For that matter, her entire body felt as if it was on fire. "I guess we had better go in."

They strode up the sidewalk arm in arm. Clover unlocked the front door and they went in. Will closed the door and immediately reached for her. He positioned her up against a wall and lifted her skirt. His kisses were hot and urgent, and his fingers between her legs were almost instantly replaced with something much larger.

She gasped. "Will!"

"Tell me you like it."

"I do . . . don't stop."

"Tell me you love me."

"I love you. I adore you." She panted.

It was fast and rough and over in minutes, and Clover swore she saw stars as the final bliss struck her. Weak, flushed and breathing harshly, she leaned against the wall while Will recouped some of his own strength.

When he released her, she stumbled to the bathroom, then put her hands on the sink counter and let her head fall forward. Each time was better than the time before. How that could be was a mystery, but Will never ceased to amaze her. She hadn't anticipated so much eagerness from him so quickly, although she herself had caused it by teasing him in the car.

She raised her head and looked at her reflection in the mirror. It was unbelievably easy to arouse Will. To arouse herself. They were going to have an incredible life together.

Sighing contentedly, she turned on the water faucet.

They ate, they made love, they called Billy and Francine to tell them about their engagement and they made love again.

By evening, they were both in a mellow, languorous mood. They prepared a snack and took it to Clover's bedroom, where they sat cross-legged on the bed and ate.

"Oh," Clover said suddenly. "I just remembered something. You left a blue jacket here."

"Is this where I left it? I wondered where it was."

"I'll get it."

As Clover bounded away, Will called, "I don't need it now." But she was gone, and he shook his head and smiled. She was fantastic, probably the most fantastic woman on earth. He'd honestly never thought about such a thing before, but knowing that no other man had made love to the woman in his life was an incredible turn-on. He couldn't get enough of Clover; he might *never* get enough of Clover.

Which was great. He loved her madly, she loved him, they were perfect in bed, he was finished with the music business, and they were going to live on a farm. *Everything* was perfect.

She came in with the jacket and held it out to him. "Here."

"Honey, I don't need it now. Just lay it on a chair."

Clover looked at him. "There's . . . an envelope in the right pocket."

"An envelope? What is it?"

"Might be something important. Maybe you'd better check and see."

Will took the jacket. "Couldn't be too important if I don't remember it." He pulled out the envelope and looked at it. "Oh, now I remember." His gaze rose to Clover's face, and he suddenly understood what had happened. "Did you read this?"

She stood with her hands behind her back, but her eyes never strayed from his. "I wanted to."

"You wanted to but you didn't. How come?"

"I don't read other people's mail."

Will looked at the envelope again, then held it up. "Read it."

"You read it out loud."

"No, I want you to read it." Will could see that this had been bothering Clover. She'd seen the pink ink and wondered, and it seemed nothing short of miraculous to him that she hadn't immediately read the message.

Slowly Clover took the envelope and extracted the folded paper. Instantly she saw the signature, *Sara*. Clover's eyes darted to Will's. "I don't have to read this, Will."

"Yes, you do."

She cleared her throat. "'Will. Thanks for your suggestion. I called Francine Dove and introduced myself, and discovered that she's as warm and open and friendly as you said. You were right about rumors being vicious things. Billy's been like a big brother to me, but gossip was making a mountain out of a molehill and it's no wonder that Francine was on Billy's case about me. Anyway, she invited me to come and see her when I get back to Nashville, which I most definitely will do. Thanks again, pal. Sara.'"

Clover's eyes came up slowly. "I thought it might be from Sara."

"But you also thought it would be something personal."

"Will, I despise jealousy, but..."

Will transferred the tray of snacks to the night stand and patted the bed. "Come here." Clover sat beside him. He took her hands in his. "I'm going to tell you something that comes from the bottom of my heart. I'm a one-woman man, Clover. I could be a thousand miles away from you and gone for five years, and I wouldn't cheat. If that's the reason you hate the music business, please think about it."

She spoke huskily. "I'm sure Billy and Francine have never cheated. That's not it, Will."

"Then what is it?"

"I'm just different than my parents. You're different than Pudge was, aren't you?"

"Yes, I am."

"Will, I knew you didn't come from some woman to me. I knew that whatever was in that envelope wasn't anything to be hurt about. But it was some sort of a symbol. I wanted you with me and you were miles away."

He caressed her cheek. "As I sit here right now, there isn't the slightest plan in my mind to ever be miles away from you again. But life takes some funny twists, honey. We can never be sure of what fate has in store for any of us."

There was peace in Clover's soul. She was glad that she'd behaved honorably with that envelope, and glad that she hadn't pressured Will into quitting the band. Her parents were behind her; they'd *always* been behind her. Francine or Billy could have interfered, and it wouldn't have been out of character for either of them to do so, but they hadn't, and that made Clover love them all the more.

And the best part of it all, Will had made his decision to get out of the music business without any influence from her. His putting a deposit on that farm had undoubtedly been because of her, but she would make sure he never had any cause to regret it. Besides, woodworking and farming sort of went together; he'd already chosen one of the outbuildings for a shop.

"I love you, Will Lang."

"I love *you*, Miss Clover." Will grinned wickedly. "We've solved practically every problem known to mankind today. Let's have some fun now."

They laughed together, the way they planned to do everything together for the rest of their lives, and tumbled down to the bed.

*   *   *   *   *